# UNIVERSAL DEFENDER
## <BOOK 3>

# ENTER UNMAKER

BY GREGOR FJELLREV

BLUE FORGE PRESS
Port Orchard, Washington

Universal Defender: Enter Unmaker (Book 3)


First eBook Edition February 2022
First Print Edition February 2022

ISBN 978-1-59092-949-0

Cover design by Brianne DiMarco



Blue Forge Press is the print division of the volunteer-run, federal 501(c)3 nonprofit company, Blue Forge Group, founded in 1989 and dedicated to bringing light to the shadows and voice to the silence. We strive to empower storytellers across all walks of life with our four divisions: Blue Forge Press, Blue Forge Films, Blue Forge Gaming, and Blue Forge Records. Find out more at www.BlueForgeGroup.org

Blue Forge Press
7419 Ebbert Drive Southeast
Port Orchard, Washington 98367
blueforgepress@gmail.com
360-550-2071 ph.txt

*To those who know who they are,*
*thanks for letting me have your characters*
*tell their stories in mine.*

# MORE BY GREGOR FJELLREV

## Universal Defender

Book 1: Today I Save Myself

Book 2: Fire to Burn the Stars

Book 3: Enter Unmaker

## Blue Flash

Miles Radien and the Cult of the Chaosmaker (Universal Defender)

Veralis Stratenheim and the Bridge Across Fire (Universal Defender)

Reticent (Angels of Anarchy)

Talenostrum

Night of the Whapwolf

In Combat with Time

www.BlueForgePress.com

# UNIVERSAL DEFENDER
# <BOOK 3>

# ENTER UNMAKER

BY GREGOR FJELLREV

# PROLOGUE

Miles simply sat there, in that room he knew so well from the home he once called his so long ago, while the Effigy of a stronger self sat across from him, between them two cups of homemade mead in earthenware vessels.

"And now we're here," Miles started. "At what might very well be the end of the line for me, the final time I ever speak with you. You, who guided me all this way along my journey without even saying a word."

Miles sighed at his seat. "I'm not worried about dying. I'm really not. I've never feared the prospect, for a lot of reasons, many of them just some different way of saying 'I'm tired,' and 'I'm tired of being tired.' No, what worries me is what will happen to you. You're the stronger me, the better me, the wiser me, the me with no weakness. But despite all that, you're still only known to me, and you only exist in my mind's eye."

He took a sip from the cup as the Effigy just sat there and listened.

"I remember that first day you came to me, when I was

six years old... it was a real rotten one, that day. I don't even remember why, but I do know that I sure wasn't taking it well. I sat in that corner over there, in this old house we're in right now. All I could think, but not dare to say, was just how much I hated it all, but then I saw you. You didn't say anything, you didn't need to, for me to understand who you were: Me but better in every way. And you just sat next to me as I cursed the world and everyone on it."

Miles sighed again, leaning back in his chair. "No bullshit motivational quotes from a poster of a cat looking at a sunset or some garbage, no talking out your ass with the kind of words that could make me vomit... no, you just sat there next to me in silence, like no one else did."

Another sip of mead, and another confession to follow. "That was the day I swore to be like you. Because you're everything I'd be if I could be anyone. But I'm not you, I've never even gotten close to being a shadow of who you are. And if I die... what does it matter where my soul finds itself or where my consciousness heads off to? You only exist to me, and so the universe would lose you. I can stand a universe without me, it'll move on. But I think the stars just might go cold if they never got to know you."

Miles then let out a nihilistic chuckle. "You're both too good to be a part of this universe, and too good to lose. I mean, here I am, stretching these last few moments of my life out into hours in this space as I tell you just how I got here. After all, you really do need an update."

# PART I

## THE SUBJUGATION OF THE COSMOS

It started around when I was wondering again how long I'd had The Aura for, and figured out it was a little over five hundred fifty Earth years since I left that planet. But something felt... fundamentally off with the universe. I still remembered my victories, like the defeat of Avanchenvaldr, and the Opponent Unbeatable, and the at long last death of my mother, at the hands of Veralis, whom I owe greatly for it. I also still remembered my failure on Kalivan Tor, the rage that followed, and its aftermath in renaming that world The Planet of Traitors, and renaming the Siivalar the Exiled Chapter, convincing the collective Vulpian species to strike their name from the annals of their race, dishonoring them forever. The problem started when I realized I was having trouble remembering everything else. The parts in between, the minor victories. On my second visit to Orvitaire, I met and sparred with a well-to-do Loriken. I still don't remember her name, I barely remember that the outcome was a tie. I still can't remember how long I was on Nibiru for during that business.

However, I still remembered Xenidar's warning against ignoring the hairs on the back of my neck, especially with The Aura, so I consulted the Prism. At the time, they shared my concern, noting that some more remote planets that still had civilization nonetheless were having similar problems, but on a slightly larger scale. They were forgetting their history, and having to confirm whether or not something truly happened the way it did far more than healthy. One such planet was none other than Raon-Arashal, which I had been meaning to visit already. So I started there.

The Death World Vulpians of that planet certainly are a crowd I can get along with. Decidedly the more... well, thing is, I hate to say 'warrior culture,' because the problem with using that term is that it gets *everyone's* eyes rolling out of their skulls, since so many damn places do it wrong. The Death Worlders are among the few that honestly got it right. I think the big problem people have with it, Humans especially...

...All right, fine. Humans almost *exclusively,* is that they seem to be under the impression that 'warrior culture' is synonymous with 'punch whoever you want and generally be an asshole without consequence.' This is absolutely not the case, especially not with Raon-Arashal. A hobby of punching does *not* a warrior make, no matter how good at punching the hobbyist is. On Raon-Arashal, you don't *have* to respond to insults with violence, but nobody's gonna tell you that you can't, especially if the insults are particularly affronting.

Look, I could honestly go for hours over the finer points of how Raon-Arashal actually got stuff like dueling laws right, but I probably don't have the time, and I don't want to gush excessively over the Planet of Actually Really Cool People When it Comes to Warriors, For Once.

To have skill is the prime pursuit of many Death Worlders, and if you asked one what they wanted to be good at, the answer was usually "Yes." Definitely a bunch I can get along with.

There's even a popular greeting on that planet, which is the sound "Borf." It ranges in meaning from a friendly hello, to an announcement of your presence, or even an acknowledgment of what someone has said, but you don't have anything useful to reply with. So you reply with a borf. It's also a fun sound to make. See, I *knew* I was onto something with naming my sword The Borfblade.

As I approached the planet in the Aura Runner, I was hailed by traffic control, per standard procedure. I distinctly remember after the guy in the tower said, "Welcome to Raon-Arashal."

After confirming my clearance, I said, "I've been looking forward to visiting at last."

What made it notable was his reply of, "Not many say that, admittedly. But it's usually because they'll fit right in."

That gave me a strange amount of comfort. Strange in the way of the fact that it was a lot. Like, *way* more than I would anticipate. Maybe it was because I had wanted to visit for a while, and to my surprise, the people I admired were willing to let me in. It was a far cry from any collective back on

Earth, I can tell you that. That fact definitely also played a part in it.

I landed in Kendradeyne, the largest of the cities, and likely the only one that was actually the size of a city-state. Though there were plenty of permanently inhabited places, this was by far the largest and most major. The rest were a few towns large enough to be called a township, and scattered hamlets or stations near the Black Zones themselves. It sure felt like my kind of place, even considering the extreme survivalism tests that are the Black Zones. Or perhaps in time, especially considering them.

The first day, I just wandered around Kendradeyne, heading into places that looked cool, whether museum, restaurant, temple, or training gym. It was unfathomably liberating not only to do that, but to know and understand that I could, that if I wanted to check a place out, I could just walk right in and do whatever it was they had to offer, with no worry of things like time or budget.

For all the rigidity and structure I imposed upon myself on Earth, it was honestly just because I couldn't afford to be spontaneous. And that goes for more than just monetarily, by the way.

The Library of Kendradeyne was an architectural marvel, even with the backdrop of the dome that was the protective walls and roof around the city's districts and sections. You see, the place where Kendradeyne is built, the rain is naturally acidic. Granted, it's not battery acid falling from the sky, but it was acid rain, and you really wouldn't want to be subjecting city buildings to it. So from the outside,

Kendradeyne just looks like a bunch of black-stone domes connected by corridors, because the walls are all made of Dredgestone, the ultimate in weatherproof material. It has to be on a planet like Raon-Arashal.

Naturally, I had to go into the library once I saw it.

Along with the shelves and shelves of volumes, and the terminals to search for particular works, there were desks free to use, both with and without computers, some prearranged to have writing utensils ready in case someone had a sudden stroke of literary genius.

There's actually a phrase you can yell in the Death Worlder dialect of the Vulpian language, *"Rhuss kolsal!"* which literally translates as "Flood of knowledge." but colloquially means "Get me a pen and paper, I'm having an epiphany!" And if you were to do that, someone would scramble to get you a pen and paper before you forgot, or turn on a voice recorder so you could just have the stream of consciousness before the lightning strike was over.

After the library was the Temple District. At first I was a bit concerned, any city with an entire district to temples would arouse my suspicion. But that was before I had figured out how such things worked in the modern universe. Which is to say, religion in the Human sense doesn't exist. Creator deities are entirely phased out, and when someone mentions gods, they mean more 'gods of character' or of virtue. Embodiments, principalities and domains, rather than purporting to omniscience. Even then, hardly anyone referenced particular pantheons or deities. A phrase like "By the gods" was never said because you paid attention, or because you believed in them, but more just because it's an expression of awe or shock. There's a sort of... inherent understanding that 'The Gods' means as much as 'The Stars' or 'The Realms.' Different languages telling the same story.

So the Temple District was, instead of shrines and temples to named ethereal beings, they were instead temples to virtues of character, and as such, any deities that were associated with those virtues.

There's a temple to honorability, *Torvalseyl,* or "Honor's due." more directly translated. Dozens of different temples to skills, a few to the very concept of skill and learning itself, a shrine to the art of the duel, a temple to health in body and mind, and smaller shrines towards the generally nice things in life. No shrine to luck, though. I approved of that. The Death Worlders don't consider luck a good thing, because of how atrocious a lack of it can make a person's life. I actually remember reading once, that the word for 'luck' in the Death World Vulpian language is *Kalleyva-Ja*, literally translating as 'Darkest importance.' They are *definitely* a crowd I can get along with.

But it was actually the Temple District that allowed me to figure out that something was indeed wrong, because the one that I went to had people who had figured it out like I had.

It was at the Shrine of Torvalseyl that I decided to meditate and ponder, and as I approached, I was met with a Death Worlder who asked me what my purpose was at the shrine.

"May I meditate at the shrine?" I asked him.

"Perhaps," he replied. "Do you remember why you must meditate?"

"That's the thing. I must meditate to remember."

It was as if that was precisely the answer he was looking for, and he let me in, asking if I would permit him to act as Catalyst with me, since he wished to meditate as well. Catalystic Meditation is a method often used by power-wielders, where two people enter a sort of meditative debate, exchanging words and answering questions with the first things that come to mind, whilst 'relaxing' your Psionic muscles, for lack of a better descriptor, and letting everything, your body, your mind, your power, just wander and let whatever happens be what happens.

The two of us paced around each other along the circle on the floor, directly opposite to each other, that we had to peer over our shoulders to actually see our partners.

"A question burns in my mind, hot and fast, that needs be reignited constantly," I began. "This is abnormal, particularly in the face of the eidetic memory that The Aura bestows."

"Thus, the abnormality is not in the question itself, but the fact it must be reminded to be asked," my partner replied.

I nodded as I stopped in place, and so did he as we turned to face each other, and I threw out my first postulation. "Memory is dying."

The Death World Vulpian across from me shook his head. "Memory is not where this alteration lies. I know myself well enough to know that I don't forget the kinds of things I've had tendency to as of late."

Our pacing resumed.

"Memory's jeopardy is merely a symptom, then. A more primal decay lies at the nexus of the mystery," I added.

"What are we forgetting, though? What information brings such strain in its recollection?" my partner asked as he looked down at the floor while we paced around each other.

We stopped in place again as he now had a theory. "Information, perhaps? Factual truth?"

I thought for a moment, but then shook my head. "We're closer than we were before, but we're not there yet."

Our pacing resumed again.

"It is not the raw phenomenon of fact, but a particular kind," I continued to narrow down. "An unnatural force tugs at the strings of..."

I stopped in place again, and so did he, as we both looked forward rather than towards each other, and said in unison: "History."

As simultaneously as we had figured it out, we both pulled the palms of our dominant hands back and let loose a harmonic pulse of The Aura, and the shimmering wave lit all of the candles in the room in its wake. It meant that we were successful. We had come to the right conclusion.

I looked around the room, seeing all the candles having lighted, before I finally spoke again. "Sometimes I hate being right."

To this, my partner nodded in mutual sentiment. "I know the feeling."

My new friend on Raon-Arashal, by the name of Keldar, intended to relay this conclusion to those it mattered to, and I agreed that was a good idea. In knowing what the problem was, this gave a baseline defense against it. With Raon-Arashal imminently vigilant, I spent a final few days on the planet before making my next move.

I found myself frequenting a place called the Warrior's Gate, and found my new favorite drink: The titular cocktail that the place was named for. And in an area literally designated as the 'Mysterious brooding corner,' I did a lot of pondering. I'm serious, there was a sign and everything.

*Rules of the Mysterious Brooding Corner:*

*If you are sitting on your own at a table in the Corner, you must brood mysteriously until someone approaches and sits across from you. After that... well, we don't know what'll happen next. We're warriors, not oracles.*

Whether ale or Warrior's Gate, I was finding myself staring into the glass like it would give me more answers than my own mind could. I only wasn't talking to you then because it was a public place, and I didn't want to look *too* crazy. But even then, I felt an odd sort of silence as I questioned what the hell was wrong with the universe, like the kind you feel when you find out that someone you once looked up to turned out to be a horrible person, or when you see yet another reason why everything has failed, nothing is good anymore, and your lifetime is cursed. That sort of emptiness that you can't even muster the will to be angry at, because it's happened more times than can be counted, and all you get out is a weary 'fuck you, go away,' hoping that in not having an interesting reaction, all the bullshit will just lose interest in you and let off. And yet, the universe has naught but the disturbing will to keep kicking anyway, even though it has no right to keep being so amused by it. Eventually, you start to figure that all life is just constantly saying 'Well, there goes another one' constantly and constantly until you can finally die yourself, and maybe hope that the next realm doesn't consist exclusively of people you once thought highly of turning out to be monsters, and people who already were. But I wouldn't hold my breath on it, to be perfectly honest.

I felt that surreal dread as I thought about the strange phenomenon that I had encountered, with history itself being in a slowly-creeping danger that I felt powerless to stop. Because it was moving just that slow, slow enough to never be properly realized until it was too late, and the pace it moved at was the pace it always would. For the first time in a while, I felt like I was back on Earth. And that's *not* a good feeling. I never want to feel like I'm back on Earth, no matter how long The Aura lets me live for.

I was on Raon-Arashal, dammit! I was exactly where I wanted to be, and yet... what kind of person does that make me? If I can't get away from how crap I feel even after I've got everything I wanted, what kind of rotten soul does that reveal me to be?

My only solace was that properly shitty people never have this debate. A third Warrior's Gate and two pints of amber ale were down the hatch, and the hot meal I had ordered. The Aura's capability to slow inebriation is pretty great, I'll admit.

I suppose in a way, this was also helpful. I only say that because a Death Worlder sat across from me and commented that I was brooding mysteriously like a pro, and he was very impressed. He also noted that there was no way I was taught how to do it, and that I must've come from a pretty dull place if I had this much natural skill at it. We had a good laugh as we riffed off of each other for a bit. What a guy. Not long before I left, he then asked me what was eating at me so hard, so I told the truth.

"It seems history itself is in danger. The worlds are forgetting their victories and heroes, albeit very slowly. Nobody's forgotten about Kennan Ironbork or the Defenders, but some smaller things... a bout won here, a successful defense against a superior force there, who it was that invented that thing elsewhere, they're in... well, flux, for lack of a better word. Like the recollection of these things is shuddering and shaking like they might vanish or change."

The Death World Vulpian across from me thought for a moment. "I think I see it," he said. "It is indeed surreal. Have you considered checking more... remote planets? Places where that sort of thing may not have originated, but could definitely be more present if only for their remoteness?"

"A sound idea. I'll do that next, once I finish this drink."

He then shook his head. "Not immediately, you're not. First you gotta have some fun here. And... you're the guy who fought those one-man battles in Hulae and Tahrengard, right? Well, Kendradeyne's open martial tournament is in two days, and the winner gets an invitation to the planetary."

I nodded my head, slowly at first, but then more vigorously as I thought about it. A Martial Tournament is slightly different than a Martial Arts Tournament in most places, despite the similarity in name. The latter is ring fighting by a set of rules per the art itself, and the former, that I was finding myself eager to enter, was an arena of twenty to thirty people in a free-for-all until one person was left.

After finishing up at the Warrior's Gate and paying in the form of a promise to play guitar next time I came, I went to the place where the registration was being held. Since this was only city-level, there was only going to be one round's worth of competitors, and nineteen others had put their name down for it. I signed my name at the registrar, and made my way into the preparation and staging area. I was soon approached by a Vulpian officiator, specifically one of the Bendorkin Chapter.

"Miles Radien? You're up for armament selection."

I followed him to an area where there was actually just a bunch of sticks that had been seemingly picked up from the ground by someone who thought they looked good. But I was ready for that, I had read the rules and knew what I was getting into.

"Grab the one that looks best to you, and head to platform seven," the officiator instructed. "Much as you might be more comfortable with your own steel, this is a competition, and one to the yield or knockout. Whichever comes first."

I nodded, and studied the sticks, immediately grabbing one that I knew just sang to me. The officiator then nodded, and commented, "You've got a good eye for sticks."

I could only respond, "Comes with a solitary

upbringing, and an active imagination."

He silently concurred as he led me to my staging platform. Once everyone was ready, a voice came over the area to brief the competitors.

*"The biome of today's arena is: Temperate Mountain Forest, day. Skill guide your paths unto victory."*

I suddenly found myself in the middle of a forest reminiscent of the kind I had hiked through near the Cle Elum River in Washington. A flat-ish area with a ground covered in packed twigs, dirt and leaves, and spaced-out century-old trees. Granted, the main difference was that it was thankfully not the Cascade Mountains themselves, which are undoubtedly among the most contemptuous bastard piles of rock I've ever had the misfortune of navigating.

Fortunately, this was only a Holographic Arena that *looked* like that area. Stick in my left hand, I started moving forward with caution. I then turned around and side kicked one of the trees, and with my enhanced strength from The Aura, shook it pretty good. A few seconds later, a guy fell flat on the ground next to me as I pointed my stick at him and he yielded, saying, "All right, fair enough. I yield." He then was warped out of the arena. I've always had good hearing, even before The Aura.

I saw two people engaging each other not far from me, but had no intention of getting victory through cowardly tactics. I jumped up a few rocks to get a better look at the area.

I suddenly found myself in an oddly meditative state immediately after that. The specific act of just hopping right up onto the higher hill brought back a flood of memories of doing the same in my backyard all the way back on Earth... but now, I was really there instead of just imagining it. I could even see that same rock wall I'd jump up to get a vantage point over illusory foes.

And so I was suddenly back in the paces, parrying and riposting incoming strikes from whoever dared stand against me, and back in the real world on Raon-Arashal, everyone was converging on each other. The hyper-practical strikes and parries I used to do gave way to a more fluid set of motions and turns that still struck true, just with that extra bit of skillful flair to them. Though this was no excessively 'fancy' style, it was still more... well, how would I describe it? I wasn't flipping and spinning about constantly like a Wushu wannabe who saw too many movies, but by the same token, I wasn't just locked into the same one-two-three combo over and over again. I had finally realized that I was supposed to be having fun in my adventuring. And so I moved opponent to opponent, ducking, weaving and turning as I blocked, parried, slashed, swiped and thrust away, just like all those fantasies had me doing. But now they were real. Now I was actually doing it, and that only served to make me fight harder and with more enthusiasm and vigor.

My last two opponents decided to team up on me, hoping to knock me down, then duel each other. But as I backed up and fended off their attacks, I was in the zone. Once my foot hit the rock wall, I pushed off and jabbed one in the gut, stunning him as I then grabbed the other guy's arm and pulled him in front of me, just as his temporary ally smacked where I was right atop the head, but I wasn't there. My living shield was. He warped out in submission, to be treated for his minor injuries.

The exchange continued, and ended as I trapped the last one's stick, and brought mine right up against his throat, and he declared his yield.

As we backed off of each other, he then said, "Congratulations on your victory. You earned it."

"You fought well," I told him. "You were a worthy opponent."

In the after-party, where all the competitors gathered for friendly drinks and food, I was told the date and location of the Planetary Tournament, the winner would go to Orvitaire to vie for the title of Champion of Orvitaire, the single most prestigious accolade a martial artist can receive in the known universe. The fact that I won Kendradeyne's division qualified me to enter in the Planetaries for Raon-Arashal.

The days on Raon-Arashal, while fun while they lasted, did very importantly confirm that something was up. But I more or less needed to wait and see where else this might be popping up, and I'm not fond of wait-and-see approaches in any regard, especially in a place as big as the universe, that quite honestly should be big enough to not have to wait around for something to happen in.

I looked at more outlying planets in clusters and galaxies, places where there wasn't a whole lot going on, because that's where someone who's planning something big would start. If they had the resources and time, they'd experiment on a planet close enough to the mainstream to be in decent spitting distance, but far out enough to not be noticed by the casual eye, and even some prying ones.

I have always known that if you're not looking, you really don't notice shit. I mean, sure, it's kinda obvious, especially on Earth, where you could swap your whole damn wardrobe in public, and the mere fact that it was in public made sure you were undetected. But The Aura really is a hell of a thing, for lack of better terms.

My impromptu advisor on Raon-Arashal was right, though. I did find what I was looking for on a planet called Zendravas, a 'refuge world' as it was classified. Basically, a Refuge World is a planet that you go to if you're not planning on heading back. Refuge Worlds exist entirely for those who need to live a life of few people, for whatever reason. Maybe they ran from something, someone, or past actions that they truly wish they could find absolution for, but never would have it, and suicide wasn't an option. Sometimes they're called 'Exile Worlds.' Either way, I had been doing these deep-field scan pulses on galactic rim areas, looking for out-of-place energy, and Zendravas gave me the ping.

If I was anyone else, I would've stayed on Zendravas for the rest of my life. I really would've. If I was the same person I was back on Earth, this would be where I'd go. It was exactly what the nomadic introvert wanted. People only getting involved in very essential stuff, whatever literally could not be done with only one set of hands. And also only when you asked. That would've been a gift from the gods for Old Earth Miles Radien. Help only when asked for, a mutual respect for the reason we're all here, and that agreement to live and let live. What a dream, eh? But I digress.

The other thing that made Zendravas a prime target for whatever was going on was the fact that due to the nature of a Refuge World, people *really* don't like being asked questions. See, you could smell the dark past on someone like my father, but you had to at least be in eyeshot of him to do that. The whole planet was rife with that sort of deal, and everyone on it. So questions of just about any regard *will* be met with skepticism and inevitable hostility. And they're not really wrong to act that way, to be honest. Perfect cover that makes sure no one actually gets to look for what you're doing.

I think my edge was in that I could relate to these guys. Most of them were Varok-Torividan. I actually recall hearing about a Varok-Torividan ship that crashed on Earth once, and that's why we got the myths of the Naga. It's actually not uncommon for that sort of thing to just... happen on planets. Species ends up crashing ship, accidentally becomes mythologized by locals. Either way, Varok-Torividan, Lorikens, assorted Kanikai and Hykentiu. There was a bit of everything and everyone on Zendravas. The majority was Varok-Torividan, though.

I knew I couldn't just start asking if weird things were happening on the planet. As much as I would be telling the truth that I wasn't a bounty hunter or someone from someone's past, that is honestly what they all say. I started by landing the Aura Runner a fair distance from any town. Landing in a town is a display of power, a challenge. Land outside, and you might just be there to use the facilities as intended.

Believe it or not, asking if there was any help that needed be done around town was a great way to get the 'new person' jitters off of everyone. I just put myself in the shoes of me back on Earth. If I was escaping the old grey I was living, and found a remote town where I wanted no one to follow me to, how would I make sure I could stay?

Prove that I'm useful, obviously.

What reminded me of why I was on Zendravas, though, was the fact alone that I had to remember why I was on Zendravas. Two days had passed since my arrival, and in them I had forgotten that I was supposed to be investigating what the hell was going wrong with memory as a phenomenon.

That's when I started that practice of reminding myself, every two hours, on the dot, that something was going on, and I needed to find out what. And when I wasn't actively telling myself that? I was making that fun little noise from Raon-Arashal to keep me in check, and make sure I was still me. Borfing to not forget. This was where I was the most thankful that The Aura made me not need sleep. For me, sleep was the black hole of my ideas. If I had an idea that needed to last the night, I'd have to write down as much as I could and leave that window open on my computer before actually letting myself go to bed. Otherwise, it was a fifty-fifty shot, weighted against me whether or not I'd remember.

I started scanning the area for anything that shouldn't be there, Psionically speaking. That thing had to work for a whole day non-stop just to figure out that yes, there was something up here. It was like the machines were having trouble remembering what they were supposed to do as well.

I had to get old-school with tracking the source. The scan gave me an area where the energy was appearing, and I had already told it to figure out just what that energy was. Didn't want to break the thing by asking it to multitask, given the circumstance.

Within the area, I would just walk around it, counting my steps as I went. As soon as I realized that I lost count, I'd mark that exact position I was standing in. This allowed me to narrow down further where this sort of memory filter was most prominent. After that, it was just narrowing it down, landmark by landmark.

Where I ended up was almost comical. I never thought I'd see a limestone cave in the middle of a moor ever since when I cleared one of Demons and undead in that old computer game. Some things never change, eh? It had been hollowed out by raw power, it hadn't been there for long. Yet it looked exactly like an ancient limestone cave would, and if it weren't for what traces were left, I might not have been able to tell.

You know how my Keystone Forge would be able to create an exact replica of a twenty year old minivan, all the stains and all the weathering in their exact sizes, places and compositions, all the scratches on the paint to an atomic level? But it just wouldn't be the same, despite how in literally every other aspect than time existent, nothing was different? That cave was like that. An ancient cave that only had been around for a few days.

The power that excavated it wasn't the same power that was causing all that memory trouble, but it was there. I found myself just admiring the stalactites a few times before I caught myself doing just that. Just like how I'd found the place, I kept track of the moment I realized I had forgotten. I don't even remember how long it took me to find what I did there. And what I found was proof.

Something indeed was eating away at the ability to remember and recall on Zendravas. This... device, a little pyramid-shaped crystal in a high-tech metal housing that acted as an amplifier. I almost forgot to write down the actual frequency the energy was oscillating on, *and* to take the damn crystal. The thing was potent, and I needed to know more about it, who put it there, and why. Constantly reminding myself consciously of what I needed to do wasn't easy with this accursed crystal in my hand, so I fabricated with The Aura a containment device. It made things a hell of a lot easier.

Eventually, I got back to my home on Cynofrax. Veralis didn't seem to have noticed the alteration to memory that I did, but I don't think she was actually being affected. Cynofrax is one of the strongholds of the universe, so to speak. Naturally, it would be one of the last places to start getting hit by that memory... not wipe, but replacement. Some nagging feeling told me that just making people forget things was only the first step. Maybe it was my analysis of the crystal that really got that jogging. More likely, it was when I realized I made a terrible mistake bringing it to Cynofrax.

I wonder if that was part of the plan. Get some idiot to find out what's going on and bring it to a planet like Cynofrax or Redaria Prime for more answers, and the vampire was just invited into the house. It was when Arakai asked me if I remembered where we encountered the Time Ender. Apparently he was aiding some scientists out of Korvideyl Station with Time Enders and other potentially extradimensional beings. We encountered the Time Ender on Homphalion, in the city of Reynvol. But Arakai couldn't remember either for the life of him, and one doesn't just forget an encounter with something like a Time Ender.

In my panic, I destroyed the crystal. Took it off the planet in the Aura Runner, jettisoned it into space, and blew it up with the ship's cannons. I'm not sure if that was as much a mistake as I thought it was two days later, but it also very well might have delayed what... inevitably happened to Cynofrax, like almost every other civilized planet in the universe. But more on that later. The crystal was destroyed, and the threat very temporarily neutralized.

I was more or less back on square one, barely having actually figured out anything beyond the proof that there was something wrong, and there was an intelligence behind it. But with the actual energetic frequency of the crystal I did have, I could find another on a different planet being affected by the memory troubles. The planet I eventually found was Sro'Galas, another 'keep to yourself' kind of world. The main difference between Sro'Galas and Zendravas, however, was that Zendravas was the only habitable planet in its entire solar system, but Sro'Galas is part of the Altorivian Stride, with the home worlds of both the Taigron and Lysanarr peoples. Gelvetori, Elas'Sotheel and Belariq... three major worlds not far from where one of these memory-buggering crystals were. The unfortunate consequence of this was that Sro'Galas was further along the plan, likely because its architect wanted to quickly get to these three planets.

The only fortunate part was that now I knew properly what was up. Memory replacement indeed, this guy was taking the memories of the peoples of Sro'Galas and removing all the heroes, replacing their names with his. I don't even think the Taigrons I encountered actually knew what this guy's name was, they only called him 'the hero,' because that's what he was becoming. Everyone who had saved a town on that planet, or the planet itself was turning into him, this... unmaker of memory. And that's when I started calling him that. The Unmaker. Of course, the locals didn't like the fact that I was endangering the name of who they called 'The Hero.' I had hopefully enough information to get some kind of defense plans out of the leaders of other worlds, so I went over to Gelvetori to speak with the parliament there.

They did find The Unmaker's work on Sro'Galas disturbing, and because of it, weren't willing to send their forces to the planet out of fear of their people being corrupted by The Unmaker. I wasn't asking them to do that. I was more asking them to be vigilant. If they started to have spotty memory of the people they've ever held in high regard, that was the warning sign. I told them to pass the message on, then worked on doing that myself.

Laksor was likely to be one of the more resistant planets to The Unmaker, and Jaden was certainly going to make sure of it. For some reason, I was confident that she might even be immune to The Unmaker if it came down to that. Perhaps some... goal or ideal that she had was just not something that required names other than her own. I'm not sure. It was surreal. But it was something I was willing to take advantage of, and so was she. Jaden's personal underground laboratory on Laksor became the center of figuring out The Unmaker.

Jaden started to work on finding out where the hell the crystals came from. It turned out they were at base a naturally occurring kind, but they had been modified into a sort of... extreme interpretation of their primary power. They were Truthing Stones of Korvideyl. You see, Korvideyl has thousands, tens of thousands of crystalline caverns of all kinds of effect, ranging from the useful, to the detrimental, to the downright ridiculous. And these caves ran like veins through the planet. The Truthing Stones of Korvideyl are a kind that you physically cannot lie when you are in their presence. If someone asks you a question and you open your mouth, you speak the factual truth on the matter. The only solution is to not open your mouth when the Truthing Stones of Korvideyl are nearby, but that itself can become rather telling.

The Unmaker had modified these Truthing Stones to... project a truth. To exude a particular fact that the stones themselves had been convinced of at no small amount of dangerous and unstable energy used to primordially twist them to this purpose. But how?

The Truthing Stones of Korvideyl were telling a message, and that message was that The Unmaker was the only hero. Everyone and anyone who had ever acted with valor, who ever held the line against impossible foes and won, who ever saved a city, a planet, a whole galaxy, even the nine people who bore the title of Universal Defender... they no longer existed to these altered Truthing Stones. There was only The Unmaker.

With our work on Laksor taking place exclusively underground, and Jaden and I being the only ones with access to the stone, it did appear to be that because of our caution, the locals in the small town of Kandorium themselves did not suffer the effects of The Unmaker's crystals.

A few days later, with only minor progress made, we heard about the first proper move of The Unmaker. Gelvetori and Elas'Sotheel were both now starting to turn to his cause. The tip-off came with a mass... well, not really exodus, but a ton of ships were leaving the planets, bound for all over the place. Ships packed with people ready to deliver The Unmaker's message en masse. The Conclave quickly ordered a blockade around the Altorivian Stride, and the Hajivakk were able to respond quickly enough to contain the situation. But we all knew this wasn't a permanent solution. The permanent solution would be to find The Unmaker and destroy him. There was a lot of confusion at first, but word quickly was spread that The Unmaker was a thing that existed, and his plans to replace everyone's memory with his own narrative was made aware to all.

Unfortunately, for some areas, this only had the effect of turning others even more quickly to him. The first system to fall wasn't the Altorivian Stride, it was the Nashira Strand. Someone from Sro'Galas apparently was able to get Exemplar

Kendro-Dalinor's ear for long enough for him to fall to The Unmaker's trap. With the Exemplar now under the bastard's yoke, the Haji-Son quickly followed, and that just all the shit hit the fan. Every day I was learning of people who had been trying to stop The Unmaker who were now on their side, and the Conclave of Sentience swiftly underwent an emergency dissolution. That open broadcast was harrowing as fuck, let me tell you.

"For the safety of the stars, the Conclave of Sentience has disbanded until The Unmaker is dealt with. Everyone who still has your minds, you're on your own, and gods willing, you'll find a way."

It was really odd, also, how they were getting about this conversion of sorts. It was never hostile, never violent. At least, not in the actual conversion. They'd burst through your doors and walls to tell you about The Unmaker like a next-level Jehovah's Witness. And apparently the actual name they were calling him was laced with his power. Just hearing it enough times was enough for most to get on board with 'em. I didn't want to know what they called him. I didn't want to take that chance.

Anyways, at first there was a fair amount of planets doing a hell of a job resisting. At least a couple thousand havens from The Unmaker, where one could plan what the hell to do about him. Laksor remained one of these havens for a good while, but even their walls crumbled under the weight of what they held back. Jaden, however, managed to seal her lab entirely to continue working and transmit what she found out directly to me.

Like I said about her, she was just totally immune to this guy. I remember last talking to her, she knew what they called him, and agreed to tell me once it was over and the name didn't carry that corruption anymore. That woman's raw persistence and cold professionalism is brilliant. It's like... it's like she was too busy working on her stuff to be corrupted by some idiot with a memory charm. Incredible. I honestly admire that. I really do.

Eventually, however, there came to only be one place totally free from The Unmaker, and that was Bol'Drakkin. There I met Kyrana of Tahnmas, a Draconian who was also completely immune to him, like Jaden.

Something about the Bol'Drakkin Draconians: Where a Dragon is considered to be from is entirely based on their greatest feat there. So for instance, if you haven't done anything particularly impressive, you might just be 'Kyrana of Bol'Drakkin.' If you graduated from a university in the Tahnmas region, you'd be 'Kyrana of Tahnmas.' Kyrana had earned a degree in Psionic Development Theory at Tahnmas's Institute of Psi-Sciences. But say you held the line at a particular location against a vastly superior force and won, you might be 'Kyrana of Kolnavar Pass.' The more specific the area you're from, the more weight your name carries on Bol'Drakkin.

But I digress. Bol'Drakkin was the last bastion against The Unmaker, and a few policies were quickly ratified to keep it that way. A census was taken, and anyone who left the planet would not be permitted to return, since the risk that they would be corrupted by The Unmaker was too high.

That whole time, there was one thing that baffled me, though: Why didn't they just blow up Bol'Drakkin? The Unmaker had everything and everywhere else, why not just tell all the militaries in the known universe to shell Bol'Drakkin into dust? I never figured that out. But I wasn't going to complain as we planned.

We needed to know two things: Where was The Unmaker, and where was his seat of power? Honestly, we were more intent on the second one, because we didn't consider finding The Unmaker him as pressing as finding out what was giving him all that power over memory from where. Unfortunately, a deep-field scan-pulse originating from Bol'Drakkin could only reliably reach so far, so a very select group of individuals would be permitted to leave the planet in their ships to travel to an appointed location to perform one of those scan-pulses, then return to Bol'Drakkin to deliver the data.

It was risky as hell, what with factoring random patrols of... well, anyone else. The universe wasn't *entirely* under The Unmaker's control, but enough of it was that we didn't trust anyone. Our scan-pulses also were looking for any places that were still holding out, and hadn't yet succumbed.

It was slow and dangerous work. We were definitely prioritizing doing it right over quickly, and if we wanted to make sure we avoided detection, these remote scan-pulse trips would take well over a week at a time. Even with all the ground we were covering, we hadn't found The Unmaker's hide. We had actually believed it'd be in intergalactic space, so we were definitely checking there. But no dice. This bugger was really good at remaining hidden, it was honestly frustrating.

Being frustrated that I hadn't found this guy out actually became one of the ways I kept my memory intact, along with borfing like I learned back on Raon-Arashal.

But now with the proverbial bunkers set up, we had time to start asking questions again. Such as, how did The Unmaker corrupt about a dozen Truthing Stones of Korvideyl, that became... all this? But we were throwing lines blindly into the abyss, we didn't even know what the hell we were looking for.

Even with how much space we were ruling out by way of default, we still couldn't get over the fact we didn't have any leads, any locations, anything at all. Taking a prisoner to interrogate had always been out of the question since it failed back on Kalisaine. Dude just fuckin' preached about The Unmaker until his interrogators straight-up took his side. So yeah, no more prisoners.

I did have the idea, however, of seeing if Xatrial Isenhart's Manifest of the Apocalypse had an entry on a situation like this. The only reason we hadn't gotten to that yet was because due to the arrangement that Xenidar and The Hideout underwent with the Manifest, it wasn't really available for viewing outside of Turazin. But Turazin was not having a picnic dealing with The Unmaker. Xenidar had to put the place on a total lockdown, and that included from inbound transmissions. With just saying The Unmaker's... *other* title being enough to start converting people, he couldn't risk anyone hearing so much as a whisper from outside. People got cabin fever, and some did leave. They did not return, and even if they had, Xenidar would've had none of it.

I needed to get a message to Xenidar that both let him know that I needed the Manifest, and that I wasn't affected by The Unmaker yet. The test of 'say something only Radien would say' sure as hell wasn't gonna apply here. So I took the Aura Runner over to Turazin to see how bad it was. Keeping my ship cloaked, I was able to figure out what SWEEPS had done so far to try to get into the Hideout. It was pretty extensive, and actually kinda morbidly impressive. They had first tried the obvious methods of bombarding the place with radio waves carrying the name of corruption, and when that didn't work, they went through more and more methods, even going so far as to create microtremors in the planet's crust that spelled out a Morse code message impersonating me and an attempt to make contact.

So not only did SWEEPS prove that wouldn't work, they simultaneously demonstrated that Xenidar would not be able to trust a message from me using a method I might actually have come up with. Because I would've come up with that eventually.

The Hideout's Defense Grid coupled with its Void Emulator assured that neither technology nor Psionic power was cracking the shell. If I tried to warp in, I risked getting scrambled to atoms. If I tried to message Xenidar telepathically, the feedback would probably make my head explode. So what the hell was I to do?

There's a kind of Talvas Vulpian shorthand that some

have nicknamed "Conspiracy Code." because the steps that get taken from what's written down to what it translates to make about as much sense as connecting Cadbury eggs to the Illuminati, but the raw actions can be done, however factually incorrect. There is no universal version of this shorthand, and it's said that everyone has their own version. If a Human were to make a code like this, they'd come up with something like "85Q" being a reference to the city of Undarus on the planet Belariq. Eighty-five is the sum of the numerical placement of the Earth English equivalent letters for the city name itself, Q is the last letter in Belariq's translated name. It's that kind of weirdness.

Talvas Vulpians often challenge themselves to figure out each other's Conspiracy Code, and Xenidar knew that I had not come up with a system of one myself. If I were to get him a message encoded in either my Talvakorrik Shorthand or his, he'd know that it'd be legitimate, since if I were corrupted by The Unmaker, my brainpower wouldn't be going towards making such a code, it'd be going towards spreading the disease.

I fired some harmless radiation pulses at The Hideout's shield with the Aura Runner, that left a mark invisible to the naked eye. If you scanned the shield as it was being 'drawn on,' as it were, you could see the message. Since I was firing at the shield, alarms were going off. The message I 'drew' with radiation was 'I-29,' and Xenidar indeed recognized it as my newly created form of Talvakorrik Shorthand. Since he couldn't actually penetrate the cloak on my ship, he knew it had to be the Aura Runner. He definitely knew where the ship was, since the radiation was coming from somewhere, the trail just abruptly stopped at its origin point.

The fact that he also didn't shoot down my ship also was a decent hint that he figured it out. If anyone could glean 'Manifest of Apocalypse' from 'I-29,' it was Xenidar Ralkas. It also helped that he likely checked to see if it had anything on this situation himself.

But he got it. The context of the situation, who the message was coming from, the fact that 'I' could stand for 'Isenhart,' they came together, and I had the transcription on Techbooth in the Aura Runner, which I decided would be remaining after this was sorted.

As it turned out, Xatrial's visions included a situation like this: where the memory of the universe was being sabotaged.

*"My vision thus: Where the worlds have forgotten their heroes, their fighters, their defenders. The names of the brave and the bold vanish in the wake of a scheme that seeks the subjugation of all life. There are known no heroes but the name or names approved by the tendrils of corruption, pride becomes regulated, and is permitted only to the faction of the One."*

Xatrial was Universal Defender, sure, but he was also Loriken. And it is well-known that Lorikens around this time were *very* wordy. Even today, the version of the language spoken on Sharaeine is considered to be... well, it's like space French. I'll leave it at that, in all its layman's glamour, and all its linguistic horror.

But anyway, Xatrial's visions included The Unmaker. Or at least someone like him. Now then, the Manifest of

Apocalypse states that the best way to get about a plan like his would be to use something called the Field of Unreality, which is still only theoretical. It is based on the work of a Draconian known as Arigen Concarius, who apparently was trying to create a 'save state' of a planet frozen in a single moment in time. By locking the planet to the physical state from a single exact moment, one could duck into the pocket dimension, mine the planet dry, hop out, hop back in, and the planet would be there as if nothing had happened to it. Time was only passing when sentient life was present that could recognize the passage of time. When that presence had exited, time in that regard would be reset.

It was a bold fucking move, I'll tell you what. Way ahead of its time, but Arigen disappeared one day and was never heard from since. The dominant theory is that he managed to create this 'save state world,' but was unable to maintain it after he entered and was destroyed. The Field of Unreality is supposedly the aftermath of this failed experiment. A pocket dimension existing alongside traditional reality like if you painted something on a canvas, then painted something completely different on top of that.

The Field of Unreality would be the place to make this plan happen for the reason that because it exists out of sync with the rest of reality, you could be on the outside looking in, and run whatever operation you wanted completely beyond detection. This is where The Unmaker would be hiding, according to Xatrial's logic. So now we had to find the Field of Unreality, far easier said than done.

Something I learned is that from about the Third to

the middle of the Fifth Cosmic Era, the universe was in what is referred to now as the 'Age of Archaeotech.' This was the time where most of the artifacts legends are told of were made within, and the technologies and Psionic applications being created and used by people... to this day, much of it remains beyond comprehension. So someone clever like Arigen, during this time, absolutely could have accidentally made the Field of Unreality back then, and it'd still be a mystery to us how to get there.

Of course, the Age of Archaeotech ended because of the Sentience War. The sheer amount of death and destruction and loss of knowledge had the universe in a relative dark age. Sure, still way beyond Human techs, but compared to what they just lost, it was a dark age.

Hence, finding the Field of Unreality was going to be a challenge. Not only did we have to search for it, we also had to put just as much effort into not being caught when we were outside the safety of Bol'Drakkin.

Even for how dangerous it was to be doing these missions, it was oddly... serene, how I'd be out in the Aura Runner for days and weeks at a time. Kyrana, Veralis, Arakai and the others, they all trusted me to know what I was doing and that if nothing else, my last act would be to make sure my fall doesn't screw them over. I wouldn't call it working at my own pace as much as... working using my own methods, that other people aren't constantly weighing in on.

But I became reminded of how I lived my life on Earth with how I soon began to think and live with the threat of The Unmaker. I was constantly in a state of preparation and vigilance, ready at a moment's notice to find out that one of my friends was no longer on my side. Prepared to instantly and completely strike out on my own if Bol'Drakkin fell. The oldest truth resounded louder than ever: Radien stands alone. But that's what I've always been ready for, and it's not a bad thing.

As I continued to scan for the location of an entrance into the Field of Unreality, I came up with methods and ways to make sure that I wouldn't falter. I also created plans regarding what to do if one or more of my friends found themselves on The Unmaker's side, and I even realized that such plans would be good for in general, if my friends suddenly became my enemies.

"Techbooth, new Protocol of Vigilance," I told the computer of my ship as I waited for the latest scan data to process. When it pinged to let me know it was ready, I began.

"Obelisk Directive, Variant Three. Protocol UNID-02 Iota," I dictated, continuing to think aloud, while remaining exacting and deliberate in my wording.

*The Obelisk Directive exists for in the event of needing to disconnect from and terminate all emotional bonds to any individual known to be an established ally at the time of this recording's creation. This particular variant contains detailed plans on how to neutralize any such individual in the event of their corruption by outside forces, or sudden decision to reverse status of alliance, and immediately become enemy. If this information should fall into the wrong hands, Defensive Measure ESD-Zero is to immediately be enacted and implemented.*

'ESD-Zero,' of course, being the safeguard to keep the recording from leaving the Aura Runner. If anyone attempted to download it remotely, or transfer it to another machine, a feedback loop would fry beyond repair whatever it was attempted to be copied to. This file was going to contain information on how to destroy me, should I fall. And if I did, I know myself well enough to know that I wouldn't be using the Aura Runner to go from place to place after that fact.

I knew how to jump from Cynofrax to Elas'Sotheel to Raon-Arashal and !leysa within a few moments with The Aura, a corrupted Miles Radien 'Would never waste time with a paltry space vessel.'

If all else failed, the Aura Runner could always self-destruct to keep this kind of information safe.

*Obelisk Directive Variant Three, Codename "Beacon"*

*Veralis Stratenheim is among my oldest and closest friends, the first that I made after being properly shown this universe I call myself a part of. I owe much to her beyond any doubt, and this would make it all the more difficult to do what is necessary, should she betray.*

*It is likely that the individual Miles Radien will be inconsolable in the face of Veralis's betrayal or corruption, and his aid should not be counted on in neutralizing her, as he will likely have exiled himself indefinitely for allowing the wrong one in, so to speak. She is a skilled combatant, extremely deadly with her axes Käyner and Käynvi. She is also a power-wielder, and my personal mentor in how to call upon The Aura for aid in combat and in life. This all would make her a formidable foe.*

*Veralis is also a Psionic Empath. Though she cannot*

*inherently read minds, she is able to reliably glean the emotional state of anyone near her, and find herself willing to aid a friend if they are in need of it. I do not recommend this as a weapon against her, however, as this will only incur absolute fury due to her honorable nature.*

*As such, the only reliable way I can currently conceive to defeat Veralis would be to utilize holographic technology to create constant and perceptible threats to her and any ally of hers, to put her in a constant state of combat until her stamina is worn down sufficiently. It must be emphasized that any such attempt would need to give no opportunity to flee, retreat or otherwise seek reprieve, lest the simulated nature of the battle be discerned. Another possibility includes the use of Void Emulators to drain her of her power, but even then, what passive enhancements The Aura bestows beyond what a Void Emulator could take away still would make dealing with her unimaginably difficult if she were to betray. As I record this, I also realize that a Psionic Resonance Cascade may also be able to stun her long enough to land a finishing blow, but the cascade itself would need to be of almost record-setting potency, considering Veralis's physical and mental resilience.*

Admittedly this is a massive oversimplification, but one could think of a Psionic Resonance Cascade as akin to firing a laser through a focusing prism that turned a laser pointer into a plasma cutter, albeit much more unstable. Most people actually just refer to the phenomenon as a Haywire Loop. So... like firing a laser through the focusing prism, but not only does it amplify the beam's intensity like that, it also splits it in five different directions, and you have no idea that's what the thing's gonna do. But I continued on.

*Obelisk Directive Variant Three, Codename "Tactician"*

*Jarrek Wöllschlager is a master strategist, able to turn seemingly insurmountable odds to his favor. Redarians in general are known to be a very tactful species, and a term has even been coined within Redarian stratagem known as the 'Wöllschlager Maneuver,' wherein traditionally destructive measures are used for constructive purposes. Typically, this takes the form of firing energy-based missiles at a shield to bolster its capacity with a resonant charge rather than destroy it.*

*However, Jarrek's strategic capabilities largely rely on him having the manpower to execute them. In the event of corruption or betrayal, the Velani Militarium must strip him of his title as Arch-Militant of the Redarian Interplanetary Battlefleet, thus removing his ability to command. This would carry the secondary effect of him falling into a distraught state, having been removed from a duty that he personally holds very dear. Jarrek is a Redarian of his word, and this is a defining trait of his, as such removing him from his sworn duty would likely cause him to surrender willingly after recognizing his defiance of such.*

One might argue that Jarrek would only be galvanized by removal from office as Arch-Militant, which would send him further over the edge. The issue with that, however, is that Jarrek is extremely smart. The only way losing his rank would further enrage him is if it were done unjustly. And if the Redarian Militarium were to become corrupt enough for that to happen, he would've resigned well before then, being sure to leave explosive farewells in the offices of said dirty admirals.

*Obelisk Directive Variant Three, Codename "Cragsman"*

*Micah Jorvask is a Redarian from Nathineyl, and has quickly proven herself to be a worthy ally. She has an extremely high kinesthetic awareness, and has been known to test security systems as a side hobby by breaking into facilities and attempting to steal items from within, at the request of the proprietor. Being a Disciple of Shadow, Second Degree, her ability to conduct stealth operations is almost unparalleled.*

*In the event of corruption or betrayal, the only reliable way to ensure victory against her in battle would be to fight her in an open field, one-on-one. Bunkers and buildings are a death trap for its occupants while on any hit list of Micah's. As such, to draw her out into a situation of open combat would be the only way to potentially defeat her, and even then, that might not be enough. Someone would have to be the bait, someone that Micah has deemed a threat and intends to kill, and unfortunately, that someone would need to be willing to stand in an open field and wait for her.*

I likely was greatly underestimating Micah's patience, though. I find myself strangely willing to believe that she and I are quite alike in our ability to wield spite as our weapon, and be able to wait as long as needed for our opponent to make a mistake first. I just hope I never have to find that out for sure.

*Obelisk Directive Variant Three, Codename "Argent"*

*Arakai Selendica is a master swordsman, and his skill with twin blades is extremely formidable. However, he is not as skilled a marksman, though no slouch. As such, it is recommended that he be openly challenged to a sniper's duel, with emphasis on the 'challenge' aspect of the contest. During such contest, no outside party is to interfere, lest they risk his absolute wrath. Like myself, Arakai Selendica has nothing but brutality reserved for the kinds of people who would try to stab him in the back while he was fighting an opponent in front of him.*

*A list of recommended operatives for such a contest that may be able to best him are attached.*

I still get my ass handed to me by Arakai sometimes when we stick spar. Empty-hand, that's a different story. But I am definitely catching up to him on swordsmanship, though. I also realize that I rather envy him, that cool-headedness that I wish I could've turned out to be. As much as I'm no hair-trigger hothead... I feel a great pit in my soul as I pale in comparison to a man who doesn't need to prove himself, let alone feel the need to.

*Obelisk Directive Variant Three, Codename "Deluge"*

*The Hykentiu Miirkae is an amphibious warrior who should never be challenged underwater. This man could take down an entire squadron of submarines on his own if he so wished. As such, one should only attempt to defeat him on land. Hykentiu bodies are vulnerable to strikes against the neck gills that enable their amphibious nature, and Miirkae is no exception to this. Only problem is actually landing a hit there, as he is a skilled martial artist, and typically wears a plated gorget under his shirt to protect said area. Recommend feinting attacks against the neck and switching to striking him on the foot instead, as few see such tactics coming.*

Miirkae. Absolutely lethal with his weapon of choice, a double-pointed staff capable of separating into two segments, to either be wielded as that kind of staff or pair of pointed Bastons. Very practical guy, too, especially with the fact that he basically conceals a gorget that he's wearing. It's painted to look like the rest of his skin, and made of something called Nightplate Alloy, which allows it to flex with his muscles and breath, furthering the concealment of the protection.

*Obelisk Directive Variant Three, Codename "Aikido"*

*Dorg, like Miirkae, is Hykentiu, and likewise should not be challenged underwater, unless by Miirkae himself. However, considering these two are extremely close, this is unlikely to be feasible. Dorg's martial strategy on land is to throw his opponents constantly, using their own momentum against them, until wearing them out to the point where a coup-de-grace is possible. As such, the best strategy to fighting Dorg may simply be to not fight him, and have both combatants constantly circling around each other, waiting for the other to make a move, until he gets frustrated and makes a mistake for it. However, his opponent would need to be capable of exercising extreme patience to this end, as such a conflict could take over an hour to resolve using this method.*

I've heard stories of how Dorg kept tossing an opponent of his in a duel around like that until the guy effectively forfeited by angrily stomping away. They found him dead of exhaustion a few minutes later, with only a few bruises on his shoulders and back where he was hitting the ground. Do keep in mind the guy *absolutely* deserved it, though.

I sighed in and out as I made this memo, felt… I wouldn't say 'forbidden,' but I felt a disturbingly familiar weariness as I spoke the words, especially the ones to detail how to deal with the last individual that needed be spoken of.

*I do not believe myself immune to corruption. Quite the opposite, in fact. I am regrettably… Human… and as such, more vulnerable than any of my allies to the dark forces of creation. Thus I believe this entry to be more likely to become relevant than any other.*

*Obelisk Directive Variant Three, Codename "Citadel"*

*Miles Radien is an extremely tactical and calculating individual, prepared at any moment to disconnect immediately and entirely from anyone he calls friend if he believes they have betrayed or otherwise stood against him. He is incredibly vigilant, to a fault at times, and constantly looking over his shoulder, both proverbially and literally.*

*As such, indirect attacks against him are not recommended. Conversion is also a bad idea, as it is most likely he will discover and enact extremely violent retaliation against such. His sense of honor should also not be taken advantage of, as he takes great care to make sure it is not a vulnerability of his. Miles is perfectly willing to throw sand in the face of someone who kicks him in the crotch.*

*The best way to defeat someone like him would be to emphasize the fact that he has fallen from grace, and to convince him that he has failed to an incredible capacity, which would most likely cause him to destroy himself out of shame, as he has personally testified that he would sooner be damned than a hypocrite. If all else fails, and he should be corrupted by an outside source that feels no such remorse, there does exist one final fail-safe in the event that his consciousness is forcibly replaced: If a person were to directly question Miles Radien's worthiness to wield The Aura, his power will run a check on him. if The Aura itself finds that Miles's consciousness has been suppressed, substituted, or is under the influence of mind control or telepathic domination, his body will immolate itself on the spot, destroying him completely."*

I had actually thought of and created this fail-safe a while back, just before the battle in Reynvol that culminated in my encounter with the Time Ender.

Annoyingly, I think the others started to notice that I was becoming more distant than usual, too. I've always hated it when people asked me if I'm all right. Gods, some of the ways people worded it were somehow more insulting than any curse spat. "Are you okay?" "Are you *well?*" However many different ways there were to word it, it was only more frustrating. What did these people want from me, a confession?

In all my years and all the time I had to constantly exist and be so damn clever on Earth, I was not for one single moment weak. I was not broken for half an instant. I was never not okay. But I grew so fucking tired of being steel and doom. I got so sick of having to be so stalwart and cagey, but it never stopped being necessary. I was so fed up with constantly being strong. And it wasn't like I was unwilling to admit that to myself, gods no, I was fully aware that I never wanted to be so cold and ruthlessly tactical. I'd whisper about that fact in the late hours of the night, behind at least two closed doors and only if I was alone in the house. But I would be damned before I'd let anyone else know it. How many people were waiting to jump out of the woodwork and yell "Ladies and gentlemen, we got him!" when I made myself had? How many pretentious fuckwits were eagerly looking forward to the day that I said 'help me?' And these were *Humans* we're talking about, so there's no way in hell there weren't a fair few! And as I heard more and more loudly, more and more constantly the stuck-ups say *"It's okay to admit you're not okay!"* or *"There's no shame in asking!"* or the next insipid spittle of the hour, that served only to remind me to double down, and even more viciously guard my secrets, because *just look* at how many people are prying at them! *Just look* at how many people are *begging* for you to say the magic words! I dare not imagine how disgustingly tall they would stand with a newly inflated pride of *"Oooh, look at me, I got through to him!"* they'd have if I ever let them have an inch, let alone my so-called big secret! I'm a person, damn it! I'm not some challenge to be conquered, or some puzzle to be solved!

...

...

...

Nothing has ever made me want to kill myself more than how people act when they think I want to kill myself. But I digress. The Field of Unreality, that needed to be found.

The problem was that we were scanning for what would've been some kind of entrance, because up until then, we had been seeing it as a matter of The Unmaker having to enter into our reality to acquire and alter the Truthing stones, and plant them in the locations he did. I began to wonder if that was where our error was. Perhaps he wasn't even leaving the Field of Unreality.

When I brought up that theory to Veralis and Kyrana, Veralis actually exclaimed, "Oh, of fucking course that's it!" and Kyrana put a dent in the wall with her horns when she headbutted it in exasperation for not realizing it before.

Indeed, The Unmaker wasn't hopping back and forth between the universe and the Field of Unreality, which is why no such warp signatures were being found, and why no gateway was being pinpointed with its activation. Over an extremely lengthy process, he had been reaching out with his power, into the universe, and very slowly, but very surely turning individual Truthing Stones of Korvideyl to the exact configuration he wanted. According to Kyrana's initial calculations, it would've taken about a hundred thousand years per stone. And information suggested that there were twelve stones created.

"Even with only one stone fully converted, that's all he'd need," Kyrana noted. "If he knows what that stone needs to be doing to get this effect, all he has to do is just get the energetic manipulation from point A to point B. After that, all someone would have to do is wander past it and get sucked right into the lie."

So now our goal shifted from finding the entrance, to finding out how to make one. Scans would continue, but with new parameters to factor in our findings.

As our scans continued to do their jobs, I remained on

Bol'Drakkin more often than not to sort out trouble, that was *always* instigated by religious nutters who were trying to take advantage of the situation. Bol'Drakkin was one of the last bastions indeed, but that didn't make the Draconians there any sort of 'chosen ones,' unlike what some tried to preach. Let me tell you, there were some impressive leaps in logic that were made as the extremists and crusaders alike tried to tell the Dragons, the Loriken, the Humans, the Hajivakk and the Vulpians on Bol'Drakkin that they were there because some breathless and formless god had chosen them to be the champions of the King Is-Not and his army of the Never-There.

However many times people rightfully rejected these false prophets and species supremacists, sometimes they gained a foothold, and it was always my genuine honor to put them down. I had no shortage of flair on it, too. There I was, between a lynch mob and their target with my sword held towards them, and I'd declare "Under my protection!" challenging them to meet their god of racism. Well, I suppose it was more speciesism in this case, but all the same. They rarely had the kind of courage to meet me head on. The ones that did? I'd fight them, I'd duel them. I'd let them challenge me to single unarmed combat, and I'd beat them handily. I'd tear them apart, and their friends would look so surprised that their imaginary god didn't protect them. I never got tired of that.

There was one, though. One son of a bitch who was elusive as all hell, and I even wondered if he had outside help. His name was Porscos. And he honestly deserved that name, that sure as hell sounds like a villain's. You could just look at a guy like that and know that he was there for the sole purpose of infiltrating and sabotaging what you worked so hard to build. There was a guy who loved nothing more than to look at something genuinely good, and unironically think to himself: "That needs to be destroyed. It's too good. I don't like how good that is." And he was Human, because of course he was.

There was a not insignificant Human demographic on Bol'Drakkin already, and for a good while, there was nothing wrong with that. The Humans on Bol'Drakkin were there by choice, and supported the way of living that the Dragons and the other species there lived. In fact, there were even Humans that were part of the Jurovendr Clan-Family, one of the most respected of the lot. "Jurovendr" roughly translates to "Brightwinged," by the way.

I had nothing but respect for the Humans that were accepted as Jurovendr. They passed the tests, and in the eyes of Bol'Drakkin, that made them Jurovendr, so I was only willing to observe that as well, seeing as if I weren't me, I'd probably be among them, doing all in my power to be anything but what I was unfortunate enough to be born as. The Jurovendr valued truthfulness, honor, and strength in all forms. If a Human could abide by that, they were better than Human in my eyes, though admittedly, 'better than Human' isn't exactly a high bar.

But problems were starting to plant their feet in the ground, and we were learning very quickly which of the Humans on Bol'Drakkin clearly shouldn't have been allowed there. I decided to focus entirely on dealing with them, so that our resources weren't as scattered between keeping The Unmaker out, and sorting the idiots within.

Porscos continued to find allies among the Humans, and to my surprise, some actually were funneling me information about where they were meeting, which businesses were friendly to them, and other stuff. I kept their names secret, and was ready to vouch for them once this was over. Even though there were Humans that were Jurovendr, it always still surprised me when they acted honorably, let alone in the interest of the greater good.

And for all the strife The Unmaker was causing, I cannot ignore the fact that this time also gave me my single favorite fight I've ever fought.

It was one of the bars that served as a hub for Porscos's zealots. They let me in the door because they didn't recognize me as Miles Radien, what they saw was a Human who seemed to know what we were all there for, and that's all that mattered to them. That lasted all of about a minute as I walked in, not bothering to sit at the counter because I knew what needed to go down, and there wasn't a whole lot of time to waste on formalities. As the crowd started to realize who was walking among them, all eyes were on me and I said those eight words to kick things off right. "I won't even use The Aura for this."

That was the cue they were waiting for. We all knew where this needed to go, and by the gods, we'd go there. The first few were the easiest, they were the ones that had actually been drinking, and in chess, the pawns go first. About a minute in, Veralis walked through the door like she was waiting for the best moment to do so, and everyone froze, including me.

She drew her axes, and threw them onto the ground, declaring "Yeah, I'm not gonna need these," and rolling her sleeves up as the fight resumed, and we were in the zone.

We had run simulations in competition with each other before in the Holographic Arena, but this was different. We were raw synergy given form in this one. We just... *knew* where we were and when to do what. I saw Veralis out of the corner of my eye disarm a guy with a knife and throw it into the chest of one who was charging at me. I pulled that knife out, and threw it into the head of some asshole who was trying to sneak up on her. I'll never forget that moment. *That* was fucking cool, and it just motivated me to fight even better with her around, for the promise of more insanely awesome moments like that.

The last minute of the fight was pure cooperative catharsis, all ending with us both roundhouse kicking the last guy in the head at the same time, basically making a sandwich out of his skull with our boots as the bread. I know it sounds a bit morbid and gruesome, but remember that the guys we just iced were the kind of scum you'd think would've been forced to stay on Earth in their deep south hovels of shitty ideals and cherry-picked bible verses tattooed on their arms, when Leviticus actually very explicitly forbids tattoos. You could just *hear* Flogging Molly's "Devil's Dance Floor" in your head as we laid waste to those guys.

Veralis Stratenheim... if I had to describe her with a single world, it'd be "Impossible." Her blades are as sharp as her mind, and her voice is as kind as it is wise. With one hand she is doom upon her foes, and with the other, she pulls you to your feet and tells you that today is not your final day. I am honored to call her my ally. I remember the conversation that took place just afterwards as we looked around the utterly trashed former haven of evil.

"That was fun," I started. "That was a lot of fun."

"We still don't actually know where Porscos is, though," Veralis reminded me.

"I don't even care, *that was fun,*" I reiterated. "Also, your entrance was awesome."

But Veralis was right, I still had to find and kill Porscos before he usurped all of Bol'Drakkin and handed it to The Unmaker on a silver platter. And with no witnesses left at that bar, I still technically had another chance to infiltrate them, or at least gain the information I wanted before killing whoever gave it to me so he couldn't warn his friends.

That's basically what happened. I was walking down those streets that I knew had Porscos's allies, and one called out to me asking if I was with him. I gave the response, and he told me there was to be a demonstration the next day, where they would parade through the main street of the town with weapons held high, and taking the place over de facto. I told the guy he could expect to see me there. And I was there, across from them, guitar in hand, and amp on my belt. I was ready to meet them with blade and bolt, but first I had to tell them what they were.

I played the guitar solo and final chorus of Sabaton's *Primo Victoria* at the crowd of Humans, and the onlookers on the sidewalk too scared to stand against them.

I unbuckled my belt where my amp was resting, and set it down with my guitar, then drew my cutlass. I looked around me and saw no Human ready to fight beside me, so I said, "It would seem Radien stands alone, once again," because I did. I shouted Valhalla, and charged with fury. To my surprise, everyone followed. Everyone charged with me to meet the scum, and we crushed them utterly like the bugs that they were. Unfortunately, Porscos was not here at this demonstration. But if nothing else, he lost a hell of a lot of followers. I was willing to take that. Just like on Killentarn, there's a finite number of people whose names are part of the cause, and that number can only go down.

That was a good day.

Porscos still needed to be properly found and dealt with, and with the bulk of his cultists dead or wounded beyond usefulness, it would be trivial to track him down, and I insisted that I be the one to end him. There was not as much resistance to this idea than I expected, but then again, what Humans were on Bol'Drakkin that weren't Porscos's drones wanted him gone just as much as I did.

I did find him, and it wasn't all that hard. The paper trail was only obscured by the fact I had eliminated his bulwark of idiot friends first. But now that he was all that was left, all I had to do was listen to the grapevine. He was holed up in a house he had quickly thrown together over an artificially created cave outside of town, just a mound with an opening, and walls of gold. Apparently he had gotten hold of some fabrication equipment and tried to make a base for himself. It looked like... well, I mean, it was basically a solid gold, rough dome over the cave. It looked like a day one project when you had creative mode on. All the resources at your disposal ad infinitum, So you make a big cube out of the rarest material because you have no imagination.

When I saw the crosses adorning the walls as I walked in, I knew I was going to enjoy what I was about to do. He didn't even notice me until I got to his bedroom. He stood up in shock from his desk, and I'm not sure how to describe the noise he made... it was like a trembling screech, seething with the entitled rage of the man-child he was. It's hard to describe, but you knew that noise when you heard it, and you *knew* that this kind of person would make that noise.

I just stood there as he shouted, "No! No, no, no, no, no! You can't be here! I order you to begone!" in that ridiculous tone. I was reminded of Mirmakharnaen, the oligarch from Killentarn. I remained thoroughly unimpressed. Porscos continued his admittedly *extremely* amusing yelling, and I'm pretty sure he made multiple references to the bible of Earth. Actually... no, he didn't. He *thought* he did. But none of the drivel he was spouting was ever actually *in* the book, not even the old testament. It certainly was on-brand. I tuned him out for most of it, honestly.

I just shrugged my shoulders and told him that he was finished, he was defeated. I didn't think he could screech any louder than he did at that statement, until I took a step forward to make good on it. It was all I could do to not just burst out laughing. It wasn't fear in those screams, that's the thing. It wasn't even anger or rage, because anger and rage are the passion-born products of pain. No, these were screams of... well, the Redarians would use the world *"Rhini,"* which roughly means "A brat, when compared to a brat." It's the best I've got, I think.

But Porscos's final moments continued like this for a bit, and I had every intent of making sure *everyone* knew that this is how he died. This dude actually coughed a few times, then started stomping towards the exit door, and when I stopped him, he flailed about and barely was able to shout... well, I don't even know what he was trying to say. It really wasn't important, and I know I didn't miss anything in not paying attention.

It was godsdamned comical. I finally put the raving bastard out of his misery with a... well, let's just call the maneuver I did with The Aura a Gravity Crush, and I'm sure you can figure it out from there. But I didn't have to make his death degrading, he did that all himself.

Naturally, the news of how exactly he died quickly dispersed the rest of his followers into obscurity and out of sight, out of mind. Likely at the tips of swords from the good people on cultist clean-up duty. With that, I re-began my search for the entrance to the Field of Unreality.

I think... I think that was the first kill I've ever been properly happy to administer. I mean, one might argue that the bunch on Earth that were tailing Jarrek and his partner Brian would be it, but knowing what I know now about that situation, I was just a happy accident, and I was glad because back then, as far as I knew, I had just saved two good men. Of course, they didn't actually need saving from me, like I said before. No, every person or being I had ended the life of up until then was some kind of defensive thing, usually because I stood between them and their victory, so that was just... something that needed to happen. Action and reaction, cause and effect. Choice and consequence, they chose to keep going, and the consequence was death. That understanding always kept it from being personal.

Even Emila Stantwell, the most painful death I've ever given to a person... no, that wasn't a gladly-made one. It was vengeance, and rightfully taken. So that's not really being glad to kill someone, that's being glad to say that they're finally dead.

Porscos, though... I may not be proud of any given kill, I know I'll never be ashamed, but I am glad that I got to end him. I'm genuinely just... glad to have taken him out. Porscos was dead, by my hand, and it felt good to be the death of someone like him.

But once again now that I was back on the search for the Field of Unreality, the serenity of the solitude was able to set in, and I spent many hours in my ship just breathing and feeling the tingling that spread across my body as a result. I admittedly hadn't done that sort of thing since after Veralis moved into my home back on Cynofrax. Of course, with all this time searching, I had a lot of time to think.

I remembered that the Dark Six's servants on Earth all had an emanating energy in common, the mark of the Burning Hells. It acted as the tethering chain that allowed a Demon to remotely puppet their thrall. I wondered if a similar tether existed on The Unmaker's followers. It would have to, since under normal circumstances, these people serving him wouldn't normally do so. Even semi-hypnosis requires a constant energetic link.

I say semi-hypnosis because it wasn't a full-on mind control he was using. Mind control substitutes your free will for obedience, and whether or not you would normally do the thing, you do the thing. This was a sort of... bumping the natural decision-making process towards reaching the 'correct' conclusion. Of course, that conclusion being that The Unmaker was the way, and what have you. All the same, there would need to be some kind of connection in order to sustain the control. Veralis and Kyrana began working on finding it once I told them of my theory.

I mean, advanced theoretical Psionics *is* their specialty. If those two were working together, there soon wouldn't be any secrets in their way.

Three days later, they found not only that the link was a thing, but they discerned its energetic frequency as well, and from that determined its counter-catalyst. It wouldn't be able to free anyone who was already on The Unmaker's side, but it would make anyone currently uncorrupted just as immune as some very rare individuals were naturally. So now everyone leaving Bol'Drakkin for these reconnaissance missions had a talisman projecting a field of the counter-catalyst around them.

Let me tell you, *that* had us all breathing a huge sigh of relief, then breathing properly again. A lot less trepidation and vigil was required all of a sudden, and contact was soon re-established with The Hideout. The Talismans were distributed across both Bol'Drakkin and Turazin, and we were in business again.

I met up with Ellan as well. Even though half a millennium had passed, he had only aged a few of the years. A few life-expectancy extension procedures had him projected to have a natural span of about two thousand, with more available to him if he wanted it. He'd decided to start with two thousand, and see how he felt after that.

So, the Field of Unreality. That's how my conversation with Xenidar started. And indeed we had a conundrum, looking to solve a mystery that people with a lot more resources and a lot less pressure had failed to. Like anyone else picking up such a search, we started from the beginning with the life and disappearance of Arigen Concarius.

Xenidar had acquired entire textbooks worth of information and other attempts to solve the mystery of Arigen Concarius, and I interrupted him as he was explaining one theory tell him that the first thing we needed to do if we wanted to find what someone else hadn't was to empty our cups. All the notes and theories of others didn't exist anymore, only the information. No one else's opinions on it, like we were the first people in history to try to piece it together.

For starters, Arigen Concarius wasn't trying to get to the Field of Unreality. He was trying to get to his theoretical Checkpoint Universe, the frozen instant. One of his colleagues only noticed he was gone after he missed an appointment of some regard, which he never did. If it was on his calendar, he'd never miss it. Sifting through daily audio logs revealed that he disappeared three days prior to someone wondering if something was up, and not only was Arigen missing, the device he had created to get to the Checkpoint Universe was gone, too. But all his notes and schematics remained. Nobody bothered trying to replicate the experiment because it was considered a failure as Arigen Concarius had vanished, and not returned.

So if we could get ahold of those schematics, we might have a way into the Field of Unreality. Only problem is that the Sentience War caused such massive losses of information due to the sheer scale of the fighting and destruction, no one ever figured out where Arigen's plans went, and only later did anyone realize that no one knew where his lab was, on what planet.

What did still remain, however, was where his assistant lived. After Arigen's disappearance, all of his worldly possessions were given to his personal lab assistant, given that he had no next of kin. This assistant, a Cevian by the name of Alia Mev-Rossar, lived quietly on an unnamed Refuge World, whose coordinates were still known. The designation was STT-4-30-19-5. "S" is for the galaxy type, a spiral galaxy followed by TT, or Tidal Tail, followed by which one. 30 was the subsector of the tidal tail, Habitable System 19, Planet 5. One might call it a Kandorian world, but one really shouldn't. Kandor is the Redarian word for "Placeholder name," which is usually used to designate something as existent, but with that word until a proper name is determined. However, oftentimes everyone forgets to think of a better name, and now the most common Redarian surname is Kandor, and there are a fair number of entire planets and cities called Kandoria, Kandorum, and the like.

All though I have to admit that Xenidar seemed rather surprised when I told him that I'd take the investigation and follow-ups alone. I already knew he wasn't planning on accompanying me, he has The Hideout to worry about, but he was asking me if Jarrek or Veralis would be doing any searching of their own on this matter. I told him the truth, that those two were currently occupied with making sure Bol'Drakkin remained stalwart, boosting up Turazin's own defense, and other general Unmaker-resisting stuff. No need to add more to their plates, let alone take them away from their duties.

I spent all these years honing the oldest truth into my greatest strength, and I had to remind him of that. If I can get this done on my own, then that's one less thing everyone else has to worry about. The trustworthiness of the Talismans had already been proven, as had my skill at simply avoiding The Unmaker's cultists. Coupled together, I understood well that I could get it done myself. Come to think of it, Xenidar wasn't even disagreeing... odd that he would've mentioned it, then. But I pressed forth as always.

I took the Aura Runner to the Refuge world that Alia Mev-Rossar lived the rest of his days on. Long-range scan-pulse showed no one was living on the world now. No sentient life, at least. Wild beasts aplenty, sure, but no person had lived on this world for a very long time. It had this odd sort of abandoned look about it. Buildings and towns that nature was reclaiming were the only structures there.

Definitely a good place to exile oneself to, if they were looking for exile hides. Maybe if things didn't work out and The Unmaker took Bol'Drakkin, I'd just stay there until it was over, either by time taking him, everyone else, or death taking me.

I wanted to take my time on this planet, even though I knew well I shouldn't. It was so damn serene in its unique way, and you'd think I'd be over that by now! You'd think that in Cynofrax's forests, or Orvitaire's places of power, or whatever that I'd have gotten my fill of the still and silent! And yet here I was, contemplating just fucking staying on that world because it was just that nice for me! I mean, if nothing else, I did let myself say that this would be the vacation planet of sorts. Secret hide where I can live simply for a while, should the need arise.

I did go to Alia Mev-Rossar's home on this planet, looking around for anything that might've survived long enough to be a clue. Sure enough, he had indeed buried a time capsule in his yard. Still intact, and containing written and audio accounts of how he lived after inheriting Arigen Concarius's tools, and everything else, including wealth. Both the written diary and recorded stuff said the exact same thing, word-for-word. Must've just been transcriptions or just a want to have multiple preservations of writing and speech for historical purposes. Either way, it was a lead, and I had it.

Then I made a mistake. I took the audio recording back to the Aura Runner to get a more detailed translation, but I left everything else at the time. Normally, this wouldn't be too bad, but in this case, it was. As soon as I turned back to Mev-Rossar's home, it was engulfed in Witchfire. Burns hot enough to boil steel, and just as fast as that sounds. The house was fucking gone in less than a minute, and it was all I could do to immediately take off in the Aura Runner so that the audio recording I did take wasn't about to fall out of my hands. For all I knew, that could happen now, as there was another player in this game, one dedicated to stopping me from finding the Field of Unreality.

I listened to the single log I had as I configured more of the Aura Runner's interior, you know, the giant space hidden just behind the cabin? Four wings of this interior: Cargo, Sustenance, Training and Armory. The Cargo Wing's just this big empty space to put supplies and what have you, stock up for a siege and all. The Sustenance Wing is... well, it's a kitchen. A very nice one too, lots of counter space and organized storage of ingredients. Though it looks Earth-like in appearance, all of the cupboards, fridges and what have you are equipped with Stasis Locks, which basically makes sure nothing spoils. By locking these things into a stasis state, they don't age and decay, and thus spoil. Training Wing is just another Holographic Arena, attached to the Armory Wing, which has weapons and munitions enough to fight an entire war. I know that one doesn't need a bunch of guns and a bit of ammo, just one or two guns and a lot of ammo, but with the kind of time I was having on my hands as the Aura Runner went from here to there, searching for leads on the Field of Unreality, I wanted to train with as many different weapons as I could, both melee and ranged. I might not always have the Borfblade or my Orvitarian Collapse Rifle, and I certainly did have the time.

But Mev-Rossar's personal audio log, it was... something else.

*"Twenty-Ninth entry after the disappearance of Arigen Concarius, personal log of Alia Mev-Rossar. Petrakordum fell due to Kianar's fury following the Seven Nine Five One, and its implications. Having noticed these well and thus being Condemned in the Such Way, the solution was clear: Make like Isenhart and find Something... anything that can be Promised and kept.*

Like, what the fuck even? I recognized Isenhart, as in Xatrial Isenhart, which of course lead me to understand that Alia's logs were entirely in code. Make like Isenhart meant exile, that much I knew. Kianar is the name of the Cevian god of schemes, and Petrakordum... sounded like a place. As for the Seven Nine Five One? I was stumped on that.

Indeed it is the case that a lot of species, when it comes to their pantheons, they adopt the "Gods of character" way of thinking, rather than creator entities. A given deity is the embodiment of an idea, so gods of battle, of luck, gods and goddesses of honesty and virtue, and of course the gods of all things malicious. Creation myths are actually very rare these days, or at least, creation myths that people hold as their beliefs. But anyways, Kianar, in this case, god of schemes for the deer-like Cevian people.

With Alia's log and honestly nothing else, I headed back to Bol'Drakkin, and consulted with Veralis and Kyrana. By this time, Micah had managed to arrive on Bol'Drakkin, and we were able to confirm that she hadn't fallen to The Unmaker. Redaria Omega as a planet, however, was not as fortunate. Koros and Nathineyl were still in the balance, with Koros having fallen and Nathineyl still standing, to her approval, as between the binary planets, Micah's home world was Nathineyl. The way she put the situation on Laksor was... well, to quote her directly, "Confusing. It looks like both one way and the other simultaneously," and somehow that made sense to me, to her casual smugness. Well, more like cheekiness, which is rather standard of most Redarians, Micah a potent case of Redarian wit and smug. Of course, the fact that nobody else could glean meaning from her words would have wiped that smug look right off her face if it weren't for the fact that she had a second, smaller smug look hiding beneath it, and thus was able to maintain a reliably consistent output of smug. I think it came from the fact that her home planet hadn't fallen, and there was that sort of 'sports team pride' about it.

But we were all confused as hell with regards to Alia Mev-Rossar's log. Petrakordum was the name of a major city on Kendrossos Prime, but would've had nothing to do with Kianar, the god of schemes in the pantheon of Alia's species. But on a communications run between Bol'Drakkin and Turazin, I had an epiphany.

I rushed into the room, where Veralis, Micah and Arakai were and called everyone including myself an idiot. The whole thing was a code, but we were looking at it in the wrong way, that way being in its translation. I was hearing plain English, Arakai and Veralis would've been hearing it in Cynofrax Vulpian, and Micah was listening in Cassidian (the proper name of the Redarian Language). But the words were originally said in the Cevian language, Althrak.

*"Threithkei aekariath posarra k'e tevossoskitheir vo-Arigen Concarius, onarra Alia Mev-Rossar. Petrakordum kullth fintha Kianar-hreun k'e-Kiva-Nar-Ang-Fol, ash tevasse. Kirotho saki-vey, ash Teveiyhouhcunthal ere k'e Tevmefiri, k'e bathyhieru atae: tas-kler Isenhart, ash sier... Volthfa sall, Hierhial."*

That may not sound like a lot when I say it, but there was indeed a code written in there. You see, when I listened to his log either in English or Althrak, I could just *feel* which words of his were capitalized. Like the words were now instead names of whole phenomenons that meant all new things to him. Where there would be gibberish and red herrings for some, there was disguised a whole new language that he alone understood, which would have come about as a way to express oneself even when under a thousand circling eyes, waiting to stomp out deviancy at the slightest chance. Yeah, I guess I would know how to recognize that sort of thing...

But anyways, there was a Written Letter code in there, followed by an anagram. I know it was a hell of a stretch, but the words 'Rhivt Aktmafk Kanpac' translated from Althrak's precursor tongue as 'Gateway to Impossible Realm.' Leave it to Mev-Rossar to give a clue in the dead form of his language, eh? But the other thing that I realized was that I had seen the written accounts as well, I just needed to remember what they said. My eyes had seen the words, and all I had to do was call upon them to be remembered. The Aura does grant me a minor form of Eidetic Memory, where I can recall the events of a given point in time that I have beheld, so that I can remember them. It's like if everything I've ever seen and heard was put into a sort of off-site data vault so that my head didn't explode from having all that raw memory and information in it.

A few meditations and recollections later, we now had the written versions of what Alia Mev-Rossar had said, and my theory was correct. Where I could swear I heard the capitalized words, they were on the transcripts, exactly where I thought they were. So now we had our code, and the key. It was only a matter of time before we knew everything he did about the disappearance of Arigen Concarius.

Shortly after we actually had everything written down, a group of Humans walked into our little lab, ones we didn't recognize. They had their Talismans on, but they seemed in the same kind of trance I had seen The Unmaker's thralls in. We immediately knew what was wrong, and that they had infiltrated Bol'Drakkin, so we felt no sorrow cutting them down as they tried to yank ours off our necks.

But in the end, I put out a planet-wide call for evacuation, and that any individual not currently under The Unmaker's spell needed to get the hell out of dodge, and to Turazin to regroup. People were wearing the Talismans that were already taken. I remember those words I said, I won't easily forget them:

"This is Miles Radien calling for the immediate evacuation of Bol'Drakkin... everyone get the hell out of here. Take your ships, grab whatever supplies you can, and trust no one. The Unmaker's thralls are infiltrating with Talismans, but you'll know them by their hazed eyes. We regroup at Turazin... Bol'Drakkin has fallen."

Bol'Drakkin has fallen. I felt my gut wrench as I said it. I grabbed anyone who I could see that had a Talisman on and wasn't affected, and got them on the Aura Runner. So it was myself, Veralis, Arakai, Micah, Jarrek, Kyrana and two of her friends, those being Iraine Ironscale and Taar-Karas, and a few scattered others. Volunteers at the lab, a few civilians we happened upon while getting to the starport. Once we were out of Bol'Drakkin's space, everyone was scanned and cleared. I alerted Xenidar to the situation, and told him exactly why it happened, and I was pissed at the fact.

Jarrek at first thought it was one of Porscos's cultists, the last vestiges of his garbage coming back to try to make sure no one wins. But no, it was much worse.

Some other Human, some fucking Human decided that The Unmaker wasn't a constant and credible threat. Their ship was doing a regular communications and cargo run between Bol'Drakkin and Nathineyl, and while on their route, they took off their Talisman, but then had the wild misfortune of getting intercepted by a Hajivakk ship full of The Unmaker's goons. Naturally, one thing lead to another, and this Human had a Talisman back around his neck to infiltrate instead of protect. What kind of bullshit...

Humans, Effigy. Fucking godsdamned Humans. If all reality gets railed by The Unmaker, it's gonna be because of the Humans and their astounding sense of entitlement. Those Talismans weren't even a strain on the neck! Hell, they were fashionable too! They were good-looking Talismans! There was no fucking reason in all the realms to take it off! The logic of Humans, am I right?! It *would* be a Human who jeopardized the fate of all worlds just so they could have a few moments where they said that *they're* the ones in control!

My only solace is that he was among the bunch that came into the lab, and I chopped his hand off as it reached for the Talisman on my neck before I ran him through. So I've got that, at least.

I had Xenidar scan everyone at The Hideout, then suggested that he scan everyone when they were re-entering, which he was already planning to do, so more power to him. It wasn't a massive workload added, the scan itself takes less than five seconds, so frankly anyone who put up a fuss about it had something to hide.

As we continued working through the testaments of Alia Mev-Rossar, it became apparent that without the Conclave and a generally unified cosmos to stop them, SWEEPS was gonna be knocking at our door as soon as they thought they had the chance. The activity in that base was at an all-time high, and even Ellan was getting wary on doing his little cavalry raids that made him a popular dude at The Hideout. Disrupting operations is generally much easier when those operations can't be easily un-disrupted. And now with supply chains under the yoke of The Unmaker, the most Ellan was doing was knocking some expendable heads around.

Our plan for Turazin's long-term defense was to use both The Hideout's Defense Grid and the Spire of the Conclave's to extend the shield around the entire planet. Sure, the SWEEPS base would be part of that area, but they'd be locked in here with us, not the other way around. But the Spire of the Conclave was under The Unmaker's control, and that needed to change before any moves could be made against SWEEPS. But even then, the most threat that SWEEPS posed was as a minor nuisance compared to the shadow The Unmaker was casting.

I'm not even sure I remember what SWEEPS stands for, in all honesty. I think it's something like "Special Weapons of Earth in Extra-Planetary Sciences" or something like that. It might've actually been "Special Weapons of Earth's Empire off-Planet Sector," now that I think about it. Regardless, an only partially accurate acronym for a group of shitty Humans being shitty.

But anyways, we needed to get into the Spire of the Conclave in order to configure what Xenidar called the Planetary Lock. Both a Defense Grid to protect the two buildings on Turazin... well, two at the time of the thing being made, and another more subtle one to stabilize the planet's structure so that someone can't just blow it up.

I notice there's actually quite a prevalence in planet-scale defenses to make sure specifically that it doesn't get blown up from orbit. I wonder how many assholes made it necessary... Feels like one of those things that would otherwise go without saying, "Don't just blow up the planet that you're having trouble taking over," but then too many people basically said, "Well, it means I win, so I don't care," and now every planet with a major city on it has a Planetary Defense Grid.

Like a judgment cast on everyone who made it

necessary. But I digress.

I did have a plan to get into the Spire of the Conclave. It was a very bad plan, exceptionally unlikely to work, would be utterly disastrous if I got it wrong, and wouldn't even grant us that much of an advantage anyway. But it is also the case that I had no better ideas and nothing better to do.

The Talisman would protect me from The Unmaker's guile, but if I was wearing it, then his operatives in the Spire would notice that I wasn't on their side immediately. So at great risk to myself, I embedded a spare Talisman into my arm, carving a flap of my own skin off and shoving it in there, using The Aura to regenerate the tissue above it, but consciously suppressing the rest of the process, because otherwise my natural regeneration would've assimilated the Talisman and rendered it useless. I calculated I had six hours to get in, transfer the Defense Grid's control to The Hideout, get out, and get back to The Hideout before the thing was deteriorated beyond effectiveness. All the while, of course, I'd be in a fair amount of physical pain, suppressing The Aura's will to heal my body after something so drastically... intrusive.

Jaden had managed to send me a short video of what the greeting between The Unmaker's operatives looked like, which would get me through the door. And when I showed up at the Spire to the raised guns of the doormen, I performed it, and they let me through with an 'ah, glad to see you're with us now.' Their tone was unnervingly sure of itself, like this was obviously gonna happen. I of course, just nodded and moved through.

They asked me if I knew how to transfer The Hideout's

Planetary Defense Grid control to the Spire, and I told them yes. I just needed to access the Spire's controls so I could 'hijack the operating frequency on a Tesla Principle algorithm,' which worked way quicker than I thought it would, with them just telling me to go two floors below the observatory on the roof.

When I got to the area with the shield control, I noticed a Wide Field Energy Scanner just before the door. Which of course, would blow my cover. I knew the difference between Standard, Wide Field and Deep Field Scan-Pulses. And though a Wide Field was not as thorough as a Deep Field pulse, it still would figure out that there was a Talisman just under my right bicep, and that I was not an operative of The Unmaker. Still, there were only two guards at the door, and I had the drop on them. A draw of my cutlass and two quick swipes and a coup de grace stab later to the one I only grazed across the face, and I had my window. Sure, the alarm blared as soon as I walked into the room, but the building was fucking tall. It'd take them at least a few minutes to get to me, and by then, control of the Defense Grid was entirely in Xenidar's hands. Er, paws, rather. He's a Talvas Vulpian, after all.

My escape was simply a very risky warp over to the entrance to The Hideout. Risky in the way that if I wasn't extremely precise, the Spire of the Conclave's automatic warp field defenses might've just nudged me outside the window and had me plummeting a little over three kilometers to the ground. I'd probably survive with The Aura's power, but it'd hurt like hell and take a good amount of time, enough to get captured. That's... honestly the point with those kinds of traps these days. Delay until the point of capture.

But I got back to The Hideout, told them to give me a Deep Field Scan-Pulse to make sure there were no traces of The Unmaker's power, and once I was cleared, I headed over to Xenidar to debrief as I finally allowed The Aura to actually regenerate the injury that was that Talisman being buried in my arm. And to tell him I needed a new Talisman.

Xenidar definitely winced as I told him just what I did to make it work, but work it did, and now we had the Spire of the Conclave, The Hideout, and the SWEEPS base all locked into the same area, and as an added bonus, none of The Unmaker's cronies were getting onto Turazin to reinforce. And it was about damn time I tagged along with Ellan on one of his little cavalry raids.

With little need for subtlety or coversion considered, we formulated our plan. First, the fabrication wing had to be destroyed. SWEEPS would be able to resupply anything we ruined unless their ability to make stuff was taken down first. After that, we could move on to the armory, cripple their offensive capability. We figured we wouldn't even need to finish them off immediately once that was done, just play the long game and gas them out. But the key was the fabrication wing, as long as we got that, we were good.

And with that lack of need for stealth, I simply walked up to one of the entrances on the side of the complex, and as soon as the guard realized I wasn't supposed to be there, I just put my foot to his head with that signature head-high roundhouse of mine and kept moving forward.

The next pair of guards to cross me earned the grand prize of being promoted to corpses when, having seen them coming, I just casually leaned against the wall in the corridor they turned to walk through, acting like I belonged there, before walking right up behind them and putting my elbow into the first one's skull, and jabbing the second guy at least five times in the throat.

By the time any alarm was sounded, I was the only intruder as far as SWEEPS was concerned, and Ellan was infiltrating his way to the fabrication wing.

With the Humans being out and about in the universe, some had picked up power-wielding of their own, and with it, their own little aesthetics and unique weapons and styles. I mean, everyone's gotta have their thing. And this particular guy liked to throw spikes that bounced around in pursuit of their targets, which I almost found out the hard way by barely dodging the pair of spikes as they whizzed past me, then again as they flew back into his hands.

Ducking around the corner, his attempts to skewer me continued with those spikes ricocheting off of walls and flinging themselves towards me, but I was catching them and throwing them back. It was rather standoffish, and eventually I just baited out a throw by sticking my middle finger out into the hallway.

With a plan in mind, I caught the spikes as they rebounded, throwing them towards his feet as I advanced. This caused the spikes to bounce prematurely and take a slight detour on the route to returning to his hands, so as to avoid piercing the wielder. But by the time he had them back,

I was right where I wanted to be: Directly in front of him. He did try to stab me with the spikes in melee range, but that only got him two broken arms and a punch to the throat as he fell back against the wall, slumping over and coming to a rest before I kicked his face against the wall a few seconds after, just to make sure.

When the sword is held high, the gates of Hell await. One step forward, all is bliss.

I wasn't even sure where I was going within the base itself. I was just the distraction gate-stormer as Ellan did his work, and I soon found myself on the business end of an impressively acrobatic kick from one of the soldiers in the SWEEPS base.

I could've punched a hole in his chest with The Aura. But I wouldn't have learned anything if I did. So I decided to fight him on this field of hand-to-hand, because I respect the duel. And I genuinely wanted to see if I could take this guy on.

The first clash saw us both hitting each other with snapping front kicks as we approached, and pushing both of us to the ground. Though slightly comical, we righted ourselves quickly and continued the exchange. Acrobatic indeed, as my attempt to throw him by the momentum of one of his punches just had him literally front flip right back onto his feet and side kick me in the ribs. I re-approached, and feinted a roundhouse to his thigh into a head-high instead, and he only blocked the former. My follow-up was to actually hit him in the thigh with my left leg, and send him slightly off-balance. But as I closed the distance to follow through with another roundhouse kick, since I'm quite fond them, he caught it. But this was met with me immediately spinning around as I pulled my foot back, and tagging him good with a backfist during the turn.

See, with a fondness for roundhouse kicks comes people who can figure that out and catch them. So as tuned and unconsciously competent as those kicks are for me, so is my defense to its counter.

I could see that he was starting to get a little winded, and a tried and true combination of kicks was the next thing I started using. Front kick into roundhouse, and spinning side, repeat as needed. Definitely a more 'pursuing' combo, I'd think, it's the one you use against someone who's backing into a corner and you want to just have an offensive advance, and that's precisely what I had.

Having pushed him into the corner, and seeing a bit of a telltale smirk from my opponent after doing so, I knew I had just put him into his favorite position. A cornered rattlesnake is the most dangerous kind, and this was even the play I'd pull in his situation. Sure, you can't retreat anymore, but who needs to? Not like anyone can get behind you or to your side. I backed off, letting him come out of the corner to face me again in the open ring that was the room we were fighting in.

An explosion rocked the base, and we both went off-balance. Ellan had detonated the charges he placed in the fabrication wing. The raid was now a success at this point, and anything more was just gonna be icing on the cake. I looked at the man I was fighting, and around us as things continued to get worse for his side. A steel beam dislodged itself from the ceiling, and smacked him directly into a wall, throwing him for a hell of a loop. Out of curiosity, I looked at him through The Aura's Sight, just in case that hit was hard enough to knock The Unmaker right out of him.

To my genuine surprise, it had. Well, not 'right' out of him, but pretty darned loose. Loose enough to invite the opportunity to make it permanent. I took the Talisman off my neck and put it around his, and he suddenly seemed to enter a haze as The Unmaker's grip was torn from his mind. Even then, he was still concussed from the hit, and even more dazed from the Talisman putting his brain back in order.

I grabbed his barely conscious body and draped him over my shoulders as I carried him out of the SWEEPS base, ordering him to not fall asleep, and all I had to do was make sure not to hear anything about The Unmaker until I was home free. I told Ellan we were getting out of here, and he agreed. I also told him I had a plus one, freshly knocked out of The Unmaker's ranks, quite literally.

Thankfully, the extrication of both ourselves and our new friend went without incident, and I dropped him in one of the medical bays in The Hideout after briefly telling Xenidar what just happened.

"Granted, I don't recommend beaning The Unmaker's followers with steel I-beams as a regular tactic," I told Xenidar as our plus one's condition stabilized. "This might have honestly just been a one-time happy accident."

"One-time it may have been, but the risk seems to have paid off. He's as clear of The Unmaker's influence as you are," Xenidar told me.

A few hours of regenerative therapy later, and the guy

was fully conscious and present. And thankfully, wasn't actually a formally enlisted member of SWEEPS. He was just there because The Unmaker had him. Apparently he was part of Fortem Terra Nova's defensive army before the second Human planet fell to The Unmaker, Specialist 2nd Degree Kieran Ebensen. At least, that was his rank in ground operations.

As it turned out, he was a pilot, who just had a lot of free time at the base, and a fair amount of prior training before recruitment into the defense force. His rank as a space pilot was actually Disciple of Stars, 1st Degree. This was about the equivalent of being a *Shodan,* or first-degree black belt in piloting spacecraft. Xenidar assured me he'd find Kieran a role at The Hideout, to which Kieran was more than willing to do, heavy English Midlands accent and all.

We all needed a reliably-earned win, and with our raid on the SWEEPS base that ended with us wrecking the fabrication wing beyond repair, and getting Kieran on our side, we had it. These steps were easing a lot of load off our backs that we could now be putting towards finding The Unmaker.

But even with that, Turazin alone wouldn't be able to get the job done. We needed another bastion, one that could strengthen all the others. Laksor, Turazin, Koros-Nathineyl... and the scattered others just needed one more link in the chain for us to start properly getting things done, and I could feel it. That's when I remembered the conversation I once had with Micah about a fortress.

Kaladorum Black Zone. Home of the Devouring Jungle

and Blizzardblade Mountains, and one of the twenty-two areas of the planet where the Death World Vulpians hone their survival skills.

I remember back on Earth, a lot of kids would fantasize about what their great and massive castle would look like, and I was no exception. But with the Keystone Forge, and a window of opportunity in Raon-Arashal's orbital year approaching, I could make it a reality. Basically, that window entailed a period of transition between the seasons of the planet, where construction of the fortress would be much more achievable as the Devouring Jungle was in a state of relative dormancy as the hostile flora made their own transitions from the season of Fjaranan to the season of Kaisenar. They're the equivalent of summer and fall here, with *Fjaranan* meaning 'Burning time,' and *Kaisenar* being 'Deceiver,' because autumn on Raon-Arashal is very inconsistent in temperature, and you'll often find yourself tricked by the sun when you think today is a good day for a coat, but find yourself proven wrong by noon. But you've already headed out for the day, and just have to tie that coat around your waist and glare disapprovingly at the sky for lying to you about the temperature because you were really looking forward to coat-wearing season, because it's a really nice coat.

I may be speaking from experience. I like a good excuse to wear that stone-grey canvas jacket, so that's why I'm often hanging out on generally cooler planets, and have no love of *Kaisenar*-embodying suns.

Regardless, the opportunity to build that castle was

nigh, and it could serve as quite the base of operations in our efforts against The Unmaker, as well as future endeavors.

Raon-Arashal's go-to construction material is known as Dredgestone, which is extremely weather-resistant, even on this planet with naturally-occurring acid rain and some of the most extreme biomes civilization has existed on. It's also solid black, with slightly glowing red flecks throughout, so that's also cool. It comes from the variant of Red Dust that actually enhances the material's weatherproof properties. Kind of like how I use Red Dust in my cutlass as an 'ultimate sword oil,' an Ascendant agricultural tech named Dremek figured out how to use the compound for things other than ranged weapon enhancing, and as a result, the city of Kendradeyne was able to expand from being a larger-than-average conglomerate in the trees of Telkii Forest (*Telkii* meaning 'hellish ground,' roughly) to the hidden gem of a city carved from the perceptively inhospitable ground, a testament to the hardiness of the Death World Vulpians.

Anyways, the castle would be built of Dredgestone, and I got the schematics for it downloaded onto the Keystone Forge's fabrication database.

Then came programming the layout for projection. I had actually done this in advance, to be ready to go when that seasonal transition period rolled around. The actual castle that would be sitting alongside the mountains, that was only going to be about a third of the interior. The rest would be directly built into the mountains themselves, making sure there was more than enough room for the inhabitants, and their ships. I've always been quite surprised at how intuitive the Keystone

Forge's interface is, and this continued to be the case. I could modify a 'base template' of sorts for a castle built into the mountains, using my ship's scanners to create a holographic projection of the area that I could superimpose the plans onto.

Even before this whole Unmaker madness, I had been planning this fortress. Ever since Micah brought the idea to me originally, I had wondered if maybe I would get my castle after all. It seemed that not only would I achieve that, but I needed to. All the more motivation, I suppose.

And with new knowledge of Raon-Arashal gathered from my visit, and my heightened admiration of the Death Worlders it brought, I even had a name for this place: Torvaltyne Bastion. 'Honor's Stand.' Jarrek had suggested 'Fort Blam-Ass,' but I can't be surprised. The notorious ass-blammer of Redaria, that's Jarrek Wöllschlager for you.

Regardless, there was one minor snag when it came to the construction: The size of the castle and mountain hangar was too large for the material reserves in the Keystone Forge to actually do in a single go. Even at a hundred percent raw atomic capacity, that'd only be able to create a little over ten percent of the build, and I knew I didn't have the kind of time to be making multiple trips.

I then had an idea as I was wondering where I could go for several ten-thousand tons of raw material that nobody would miss: Earth's still-existent landfills, nuclear waste disposal sites, and the giant island of trash in one of the oceans about the size of the United Kingdom. No, I'm not talking about the UK itself.

Earth was completely under the grip of The Unmaker, however, to no one's surprise. It simultaneously meant that it'd be really risky to set up a Warp Column between the great pacific garbage patch and Raon-Arashal, while also likely being decently safe since the planet was busy doing The Unmaker's bidding, rather than patrolling its oceans to make sure the trash island was still there.

But I knew I'd rather play it safe than sorry, so I brought the idea to Darek Jor'Galn, the Arch-Militant of Raon-Arashal's Ground Force branch of their defensive army. I showed him the plans for Torvaltyne Bastion, and told him of my plan to siphon trash from Earth to fit the material needs, thanks to the functions of my Keystone Forge.

"You sure you need to get a Warp Column to Earth to get the materials?" He asked me while we were in the meeting.

"I figure it's a better alternative than uprooting a quarter of Kaladorum's section of the Devouring Jungle," I replied.

"True, but what's stopping you from grabbing a bunch of rocks from The Planet of Traitors? It's not like anyone lives there now..."

"I am fully aware of that fact, Arch-Militant. Have you forgotten *why* the Exiled Chapter is extinct?"

A moment of slightly awkward silence passed before he realized who he was talking to in that regard.

"...Right. I apologize, Radien. I admit, I had forgotten briefly. But my point stands, does it not?"

His point indeed did stand. Why was I thinking about

such a risky mission to Earth when I could set up the Warp Column on The Planet of Traitors' surface, where the amount would be negligible compared to the rest of the sun-blasted rock? I had to think about that for a moment before I had my answer, which admittedly was only partly the truth, though it also wasn't wrong to any capacity.

"I'm sure you've heard by know the comparisons between the Humans and the Elurians just before they had become a Conclave species," I began, and Darek nodded. "Though my personal experience with them makes it hard for me to believe they will reach those heights, I cannot ignore the fact that it is possible."

I also remembered that the extinction of the Elurians and the Kendrosians was still relatively fresh in the minds of many, as it had only been a few centuries since Caltoran was finally put down, and released from the control of Demonic puppeting. It was barely before my time, and I honestly did feel like in a lot of ways, I was arriving late to the party of the wider universe.

Two proud and widespread species extinct just before I came along, like I was here just in time to see the end of the fun era. My only solace would be with my agelessness, I could maybe survive to see the other side of the second war for reality.

Yes... that is what it's become now. The Unmaker, despite being such a significant part of my life now, is but one battle of the second time the universe has been at war with Hell itself, and the Dark Six.

The only thing stopping me from believing The

Unmaker to be a Demon himself is the fact that the Demons haven't started swarming the universe while he's been doing his work. What then, I wonder?

But in the moment that was my discussion with Arch-Militant Jor'Galn, I still had my testimony to make.

"We'd be doing a huge favor for them, that we admittedly have no obligation to, and they have no reason to believe we'd do it. But maybe checking that nagging item off of their list will help propel them forward to becoming the next Eluria, or when they do become the next Eluria, they will not forget what Raon-Arashal did for them in those rough and early days."

Darek thought about that for a moment, as I realized I was only thinking of Earth initially because it was a planet that I knew well, despite my best intentions, and I knew that they had that problem that could be solved with the Keystone Forge.

"We *can* do it," Darek started. "From what research has been done so far, there has been found a way to project a sort of 'cone of silence' around an area, that completely blocks out The Unmaker's subterfuge, akin to the Talismans that were created on Bol'Drakkin. I do have the men and the tech to spare, to get that sort of shield around the Warp Column you'd establish with your ship, and that forge."

Another moment passed as he mulled it over.

"And for the reason that we have the ability to spare that manpower, I see no reason not to. All right, Radien. I'll start making the arrangements. It will be your responsibility to maintain the Warp Column, and make sure it's in the right locations."

I nodded. "Understood. Thank you, Arch-Militant."

"And when that fortress is done? I'll want to take a look at it, from the schematics, it looks like it'll be a pretty nifty place."

"I'll be the one to personally give you the tour."

With that settled, preparations began. The Aura Runner would be positioned above the build area along the base of the Blizzardblade Mountains, and what trees and foliage were in that area would be used to fill the Keystone Forge's material reserves first. With the planned hangar to be built into the mountains, the raw stone that would be removed for that would also serve that purpose. But most of that material would go into the hangar itself, having its atoms rearranged into the new configurations that would be the structures and doors themselves. After running the calculations by the engineering team, led by a Shiar-Pattern Ascendant named Asriah, we figured out that indeed, we would basically break even on material when constructing the hangar out of the mountain itself.

Admittedly, Asriah ran all the calculations himself, and just about set his processors on fire doing it. As amusing as it was watching him speed out of one of the tents in the construction camp to bury his head into the snow, we had just gotten dangerously close to losing a very good architectural engineer.

"Between the material that will be extracted, and the material required to replicate the needed structures and installations, it will be about even, with a margin of error of at most, one point seven percent," he told me once he re-entered the tent, his head still steaming slightly.

"Thanks for the heads-up, Asriah. Now do yourself a favor and take the rest of the day off to recover," I told him, and he nodded to then do so, retiring to Tenbork Station, the closest permanently inhabited area to us.

The material sum of the forest we had to clear out to make the required room was enough to fill the reserves of the Keystone Forge twice. Meaning that we'd get about eighteen percent of the build completed before needing to resort to the Warp Column.

We then figured out how much time that would actually take, to determine the timing of the setup of the Warp Column itself to the garbage patch, and the subsequent grabbing of the materials. We figured the hangar could be done last, since that was the part that would break even with the materials extracted.

"What I want to be able to do is; while the Keystone Forge is using the material from Kaladorum's forest itself, we set up the Warp Column to Earth with such timing that once we're done using that stuff, *that's* the instant we're ready to start grabbing the trash, and then do so. It'll minimize our time spent on Earth, and thus at risk," I briefed the pilot squad who would be running patrol duty on the Warp Column itself.

"As soon as that starts, you guys patrol the inside of the Cone of Silence, ready to shoot down any craft that come our way with hostile intent."

The briefing continued, and the Death World Vulpian pilots listened intently, to my surprise. I'm... admittedly not used to having my advice be considered valid, but it seemed they found my tactics sound, hinted by the lack of dissent. Believe me, if they thought there was a problem, they'd let me know. Death Worlders consider it an insult to do otherwise.

"I'll already be on Earth, setting up the Column on that side. The Aura Runner will be piloted automatically by Techbooth, the onboard computer system, and will be guided by my prompts."

"Your Techbooth is intuitive enough to do the job right?" One of the pilots asked.

"Hasn't let me down yet," I said. "Ladies and gentlemen, *please*, do feel free to question my plan if there are elements I'm overlooking."

The rest of the group acknowledged, nodding respectfully for the fact I wasn't demanding unquestioning cooperation.

"Also, only shoot down a passing craft if it's coming right for us! If they're not noticing our presence, there's no need to reveal it to them! Besides, even if they do, it's still gonna take them time to scramble countermeasures, and we're not sticking around for long! From the state of Earth's tech, we'll have at least an hour between alarms being raised, and the response reaching the location!"

I then showed a map of Earth, with the location highlighted in the Pacific Ocean.

"We will be gathering material from the Eastern Patch, with the closest landforms being the Hawaiian Archipelago, and the California Coast. Between the efficiency of the Keystone Forge and Warp Column, our chief architect Asriah has calculated we'd need to spend about sixty hours planetside. After that, we get the hell out of dodge with all haste."

Everyone seemed on board with the plan.

"It's gonna feel like the longest sixty hours of our lives, I know. But we make this work, and Torvaltyne Bastion will be an invaluable asset to Raon-Arashal during our fight against The Unmaker, and *especially* after we kick his ass out of the universe!"

There was an enthusiastic *'toriyah!'* from the Death Worlders, which was the equivalent of a *'hoo-ra!'* from a Human.

With the traditional send-off, *"Skjeln thej duul'e klatars! Skill guide your paths!"* We all made our way out to take up positions, and I had to take the Aura Runner for one more trip back to Earth.

The crews on the ground started setting up the Cone of Silence projectors on the Raon-Arashal side, and the Aura Runner started its warp to Earth soon after, able to make the trip in a little under three hours with its speed capabilities, both in and out of the Warp Channel itself.

Most ships can't go above a certain speed threshold when inside the Warp Channel, itself a sort of slip-space that allows such distances to be crossed between planets and even galaxies. This is because the main materials used to make a ship's hull plates (typically an alloy called Delvonen Hypersteel, or Archonium if you're feeling really fancy) can't simultaneously take the stress of the Warp Channel, and faster-than-light speeds. But the Aura Runner is an extremely rare exception, able to travel faster than light within the Warp Channel itself, exponentially decreasing the amount of time it takes to traverse those distances.

Granted, it's probably not wise to test the limits of even a ship like this, so I only do that in very dire circumstances, such as the need to get the timing right on this endeavor.

I exited warp just behind Pluto, and engaged the ship's cloak at maximum efficiency as it traveled to earth over the next hour and a half at about triple the speed of light. My ship's cloak was able to maintain at that speed, fortunately.

The difference between an FTL Drive and a Warp Engine is that the latter always leaves a trace behind, while the former only does so if you push the speed beyond four times faster than light. With the Aura Runner possessing both, I was able to take the safer option.

Once in range, I warped directly onto the trash island itself, and ordered the Aura Runner to head back to Raon-Arashal to set up the Warp Channel on that end. Yes, it was dense enough to stand on. Harrowing stuff, I know.

I started by setting up the actual projectors for the Cone of Silence on the trash island itself, that would encompass most of, if not all of its area. Once that was done, then came establishing the long-range communications with an Interstellar Sound Channel Receiver.

Now then, the Interstellar Sound Channel is actually quite different from the Warp Channel, basically by way of its speed capability. While the Warp Channel acts as a sort of spatial compression zone, akin to distances traveled relative to altitude, the Interstellar Sound Channel is a slip-space where distance basically doesn't exist.

It's a specific point in the EM Band that if you transmit on that very precise frequency, the signal sort of 'glitches' between the gaps in space-time and enters that pseudo-dimension where any distance can be crossed instantly. It's how communications in the modern universe can span galaxies, by way of ISC Transmitters and Receivers. Of course, the transmitters are quite large and cumbersome, so they only really exist on planets and massive capital-class ships, where the distance between points is such that the speed of light will suffice. Receivers, on the other hand, can be as small as a typical mini-fridge, and are much more practical to install into personal ships. After all, transmitters typically are their own entire buildings to fit all the equipment required to hit that sweet spot in the EM Band.

When the Cone of Silence was activated, I turned on the ISC Receiver, having instructed the ground crew on Raon-Arashal to transmit on the Interstellar Sound Channel to my exact location where I'd set it up. The communications themselves were limited to percentage callouts, referring to how much material was left in the Keystone Forge as it began constructing what would become Torvaltyne Bastion.

*"Projection one, twenty percent..."*

The amount of raw material present at the build site was enough to fill the Keystone Forge's reserves twice. They had twenty percent of the first fill's material left.

*"Projection one, nineteen percent..."* came in just

under three and a half minutes later, which meant I had plenty of time. After all, they had started working only a few minutes after I left initially. The Aura Runner would return to Raon-Arashal to set up the Warp Column in four and a half hours, which would leave a little over two hours for final setup.

If nothing else, if the plan fell through, and Earth's armies started to converge on us in the name of The Unmaker, we'd just retreat back through the Warp Column with whatever we managed to grab, after which I'd just take a bunch of rocks from The Planet of Traitors like Darek had initially suggested.

After I had set up the Warp Column on my end, it was just a waiting game for until the Aura Runner returned to Raon-Arashal. Once that happened, we could use the established, but not physically opened Warp Column to get two-way communications back, as that would become possible by using the Aura Runner as a secondary relay.

But in finding myself with a dangerous amount of time to think about it, I had started to realize just how much we truly were going out of our way for this miserable little planet. Standing on Earth again, on a giant trash heap in the middle of the ocean had started to bring back my disdain for the planet... and the people on it.

These were the guys who hadn't been allowed to leave initially either because they were richer than morality allowed, or were flying confederate flags outside their homes, and were thus deemed unworthy of seeing the wider universe...

...But that first generation of rejects were long dead,

and at best, their descendants were left to pick up their mess and try to convince the universe that they are not their forefathers.

If there's anything I've learned of the universe beyond Earth, it's that it does at least give the chance. And in a way, we were getting the ball rolling with this little fixer-upper. I realized I needed to stop seeing it as giving Earth a second chance, because the Earth that spat in the hand of its 'first' chance doesn't exist anymore. The spitters are dead, whether by the sword of time or a sword of steel. And quite honestly, I'd say they're gonna have an easier time convincing the rest of the stars that they are not their predecessors than they would if they were having to convince the rest of the planet alone.

I wonder if there's actually been countless species like the Humans, with all their irrationality and all their evil-loving, but they never left their home world? I mean, I've heard that the Elurians were a lot like that once before they became such a major help to the universe at large, but I wonder if there's something, some quirk about the way reality works that keeps a species like the Humans locked away on their home world, the rest of the universe protected from them by their own inability to progress?

I suppose that'll be a question for another time.

*"Projection two, ten percent..."*

By this point, the Aura Runner was back on Raon-Arashal, ready to activate the Warp Column. With the fact that the projectors were all set in place, we were soon able to re-establish communications.

"Radien to ground team, you copy?"

"Aye, Radien. This is Asriah, we hear you."

"Status of the Aura Runner?"

"Aura Runner is present and prepared."

"Patrol Group, status?"

"This is Squad Leader Kalissar, we're standing by."

"Acknowledged, Kalissar. Await my mark to begin patrol pattern. Techbooth, do you read me in the Aura Runner?"

The AI's voice responded to my hail.

"Confirm communications, standing by."

"All right. Techbooth, once they hit five percent with the second projection, establish the Warp Column and swap the Keystone Forge to targeting the trash island on this side. Kalissar, as soon as the Column is active, you and your pilots need to count to ten, *then* fly through to this side to begin your patrol! The Cone of Silence is gonna take about that long to connect on both sides of the portal."

Both Kalissar and Techbooth acknowledged.

"Ground team, make sure the projection from the Keystone Forge remains stable! If you've got nothing to do, set up a few anti-air guns pointed at the portal, just in case!"

"I hear that," Asriah said, soon relaying the order to his team.

"Techbooth, begin countdown to establishing the warp column once we're a hundred seconds away! Five second intervals!"

"Acknowledged."

I started scrambling to the Cone of Silence Projectors,

double and triple-checking their configurations to make sure they were correct. I was *not* going to risk this going wrong. After giving the same treatment to the Warp Column Projector on my end, all that was left to do was wait for that countdown to start. Of course, once we did, that'd have been the easy part. The hard part was coming right up: Spending sixty hours on Earth as the Keystone Forge abducted this massive garbage heap to turn it into what would become Torvaltyne Bastion. Honor's Stand.

"Twenty seconds to Warp Column establishment..."

I stood ready.

"Fifteen seconds to Warp Column establishment..."

The pilots stood ready.

"Ten seconds to Warp Column Establishment..."

The ground teams stood ready.

"Five seconds..."

In the heat of the anticipation, I didn't even realize that I said my next words in the Death Worlder language.

*"Mal Kalleyva-Ja nej Aurok iln... May luck have no power here..."*

The portal opened, I hit the two switches on my end, and when I looked into the sky, I saw a hole torn into it, with Raon-Arashal on the other side, the Aura Runner between us in the skies, and what was built so far of the Fortress on the ground. A light green column shot down onto the trash island itself, sucking up the waste and delivering it directly to the Keystone Forge to be turned into the Dredgestone bricks, the carpets and floors, the furniture and the computers. The Cone of Silence soon followed, like a liquid wall of opaque energy creeping up into the Warp Column's portal, soon hitting the edges and establishing the shield against The Unmaker in this area.

The pilots descended through the portal and quickly re-oriented themselves to the new gravity they just entered, and began flying in a patrol route along the borders of the Cone of Silence.

But like I said before, that was the easy part. Now came the waiting, sixty hours of it in the best case scenario.

"Aura Runner, how's the connection?" I asked.

"Warp Column, Cone of Silence, and Keystone Forge connections are all stable."

"Excellent work, everyone. But that was the easy part."

Sixty hours of constant vigil awaited us, as I made sure to dodge the parts of the trash island that were disappearing beneath my feet. Granted, I had fair warning at any time, I'd have to be not paying attention to get caught by surprise, and getting caught by surprise was something we were *very* much looking to avoid. We passed the time mostly by exchanging banter, whilst every now and again reminding ourselves to check for where the nearest aircraft was. Despite the stakes, we had some good bits out of it.

"Telkine, you mentioned once you're with the exploration effort for Cynofrax's Sub-Ocean?" I asked the pilot by that callsign.

"That is true. We're still trying to figure out a non-intrusive way to get a craft down there, but we're close."

"Do you know who's gonna be in the craft?"

"I happen to know that I'm one of the considerations."

"If you do get chosen, once you get down there you should say say 'oh gods, what is that thing?!' then cut your transmission."

It got a solid laugh out of him and several other pilots. He mentioned he'd actively consider doing that, since he was now very tempted with the idea. With moments of levity to break up the tension, we remained vigilant for fifty-three hours, until one of the pilots alerted us to an incoming craft.

"Tailfwap to Earthside Team, proximity alert! Single aircraft on direct course bearing hard west!"

"All right, everyone out!" I commanded as the pilots started flying back through the Warp Column. "Techbooth, how much progress did we make?!"

"Material requirements have been met."

"Oh," I said as I froze in place, realizing that we had finished way ahead of schedule. "Just as well, then! Initiate emergency dimensional recall!"

I was immediately warped aboard the Aura Runner, and subsequently ran up to the helm to take control of the ship.

"Pilots, status!"

"This is Telkine, we're all through!"

I then turned the Aura Runner to face the Warp Column, and fired off a single Phase Disruptor Charge through the portal, one of the lower-yield payload weapons aboard the ship. It completely destroyed the Cone of Silence Projectors, the Warp Column Projectors, and the Interstellar

Sound Channel Receiver. The gateway promptly destabilized and snapped shut.

"Everyone, self-check! Make sure nobody got hit with the subterfuge!" I called out once we were in the clear initially. A few minutes later, all the teams responded with the all-clears.

I sat back in my chair at the helm of the Aura Runner with a great sigh of relief. We did it, and without a hitch. Nobody was lost, and Torvaltyne Bastion was built.

It was in that moment I suddenly realized that Torvaltyne Bastion was built! The castle of my dreams was now a reality, my fortress made manifest! I had promised to give Arch-Militant Jor'Galn a tour, but I still had to take a walk through the halls myself! As much as I had designed them in detail during my spare time, it was something else to see them physically, truly manifested in this realm.

Like how escaping Earth all that time ago felt so unreal for its fortune, standing in my fortress felt just as unreal for the fact that I had made it happen.

I promptly invited my six close friends to assess the place. Veralis, Arakai, Jarrek, Micah, Miirkae and Dorg were all there soon enough to see what I had accomplished. This was Torvaltyne Bastion, and I would sooner be damned than not let my friends benefit from its existence.

Remembering when Micah had told me about how the Velani Militarium was looking to find a place to cross-train at, I told both her and Jarrek that Torvaltyne Bastion might just be the place for it, and they both agreed.

"I still think Fort Blam-Ass is a perfectly serviceable

name," Jarrek commented with an exaggerated joking grumble.

"Save the ass-blamming for your spare time, Jarrek," I told him. "After all, there's a reason why every single one of the personnel quarters has soundproofed walls."

*Everyone* got a kick out of that comment. I guess they weren't expecting such a comeback that quickly. "Radien coming in with the spicy comebacks today" was what I heard from Micah. During that visit, the place even developed a more colloquial name: Fortress Borfus.

Per my word, I gave Arch-Militant Jor'Galn a tour of the place, and a rundown on its capabilities; Defensive, manufacturing, accommodations, the whole lot.

"We could station a whole Scourge Wing here," he commented as I showed him the hangar that we had constructed out of the mountain rock itself. For reference, the Scourge Wings are basically the backbone of Raon-Arashal's defensive fleet, of which eleven exist. Or rather, twelve now with Torvaltyne's space.

"Radien, I do wonder..." Darek started to ask once the tour had concluded. "This fortress is yours, its your land, it belongs to you. Raon-Arashal's Militarium stationing here would basically be at your discretion and with your permission, unless you wanted to lead this place as the base it would be, as *part* of this planet's defenders."

I knew what he was asking me, but I told him to just say the question, just to make sure I wasn't misinterpreting.

"Do you wish to join the defensive army of Raon-Arashal?"

Indeed it seemed, he was asking me if I wanted to join. Military service was something I never found appealing back on Earth. I'm not the kind to take orders without question, quite the opposite, actually. In fact, insisting that I don't question your orders is one of the more surefire ways to get me to start questioning them. After all, I end up wondering 'what about these orders is so sensitive that absolute obedience to them is needed?'

All in all, it was something I knew I'd need to mull over. I made my concerns no secret to the Arch-Militant, which he seemed to understand.

"You spent too long on Earth, Radien. That is something I've learned about you by now," he commented. "I hope I can be the one to show you how a planet's armies *should* work. But I will fully understand if you must decline."

That night, I found myself staring down a blank canvas in the shape of a banner, the kind you'd carry into battle, along with a set of paints I had created with my Keystone Forge. A few drafting pencils were on the table as well for me to draw initial linework on, and a set of brushes.

Before I left Earth, I used to make wooden shields that I'd spray white primer on, then paint a design on. Usually, they'd be used in boffer combat or live-action role playing since they were usually pine or oak circles that probably wouldn't do great in real battle. But putting those designs onto shields, and even dabbling in banners... it was fun. I even made a little money selling them for that purpose.

Now I was ready to make *my* banner. The banner of Torvaltyne Bastion.

When I was maybe eight years old, I once drew a symbol. It seemed so random at the time, a single vertical line, centered to a half-circle beneath it, and three lines beneath that half-circle, a vertical and two diagonals. But that was a symbol that stuck with me, though I didn't know what it meant or if it meant anything. All I knew is that it was mine, and it was going to be the centerpiece of the banner, the sigil that was emblazoned on the front in brilliant golden and orange hues.

Beneath that symbol, my symbol, I next drew the scripture that would be the motto of my fortress. The words were printed on the image of a scroll, the same words I had just so happened to say when I was briefly back on Earth: *Mal Kalleyva-Ja nej Aurok iln,* 'May luck have no power here.'

I continued work on the banner throughout the night, drawing the initial lines that I would then paint in black, then start coloring. Other symbols and depictions found themselves present on this banner, such a skull along the top with a cutlass driven through it.

I put... quite a number of hours into it, actually. It was something I was surprisingly proud of once it was done. That next day, Arch-Militant Jor'Galn came back to the fortress to see how I was doing, and if I'd made a decision.

I met him holding the banner of Torvaltyne Bastion, and I could see the double-take he did as he looked at it.

"That... actually gives you a rank promotion up to Standard Bearer for Command Rank," were the first words he actually managed to say.

There are basically two different kinds of rank a

person can hold in most planetary armies, according to the Universal Militaristic and Defensive Force Optimal Chain of Command (oftentimes generously referred to as the 'you mad fo' cock' because that's what the acronym sounds like), those being Operator Rank and Command Rank. Your Operator Rank within your branch and discipline is basically how good you are as an engineer, or artilleryman, or front-line fighter depending on where you put yourself, while Command Rank is... well, your rank as a leader within that force.

When Darek had mentioned my apparent promotion to Standard Bearer, it referred to how the most junior Command Rank was Representative, basically akin to an Officer Cadet, and the one immediately senior to it was Standard Bearer. In order to earn the promotion to it, Raon-Arashal holds the tradition that you must hold the physical banner of your company or squad to attain it, and I had just done that.

After a bit more review of my prior exploits, it turned out that I was eligible for the rank of Tactician.

In order to promote from Standard Bearer to Force Leader, one must have led *something.* Whether a squad into battle, or a public event. In general, leadership skills carry over as far as Raon-Arashal's Militarium was concerned. For leading the defense of Fleetgame when I started the resistance against Killentarn's tyrannical regime, I was promoted to Force Leader.

In order to promote from Force Leader to Carrier, one must ensure the survival of a third party other than oneself or their squadron in battle. This could be leading a group of civilians to safety, or carrying a wounded ally on your shoulders out of the fray. For fighting back-to-back with Synval-Kolderan on Hulae during the Demonic incursion there, I was promoted to Force Leader.

In order to promote from Force Leader to Tactician, one must actively assume the role of leadership in a battle that led to your victory. For commanding that artillery squad on Cynofrax when Alexi Erraxev made the Bridge Across Fire, I was promoted to Tactician.

There was still a long way to go before even higher ranks, though. I was already going to give the brass an annoying amount of paperwork for being penta-promoted, but Darek assured me that, "If my hunch is right about your skills, it'll be worth the pain."

Torvaltyne Bastion was complete, and I was going to be the one to lead it.

I had my castle, and so did this world and its peoples.

Jalnar Veks, the Arch-Militant of Raon-Arashal's Space Branch suggested at first that he would build the 13th Scourge Wing from the best of the best of the operators from the other twelve, but I quickly told him not to. I shot that idea down *hard,* making sure to tell him that the 13th Scourge Wing was not to be an all-star team. All-star teams fail because they rely on talent alone, and no one's got enough talent to win on talent alone. Take the single best pilot from each individual wing and put 'em in a squad of twelve to send them up against a group of decent-but-not-legendary pilots who had all been friends since youth, and the winner's not gonna be the all-stars, I can tell you that.

I got everyone to meet me at the Fortress again, and the seven of us figured out what we were going to be doing from there. Veralis and Arakai were in charge of getting the Fortress Borfus prepped, staffed, etc. Veralis would find the people, Arakai would find the materials for them to utilize their skills with. Seven of us there may have been, but that's not exactly all walks of life covered. Miirkae, Dorg and Jarrek were to work on the Scourge Wing specifically, the Hykentiu duo would be in charge of manufacturing the ships along with Asriah from the build team, and Jarrek would handle recruitment and assignment of the pilots, delegating the training to one of Kyrana of Tahnmas's friends we brought from Bol'Drakkin, Iraine Ironscale. Admittedly you'd never suspect it when looking at her, but Iraine can definitely put the fear of the reaper in your soul, and literally spit acid. No, I'm serious. Her breath weapon is acid. Yes, Dragons can learn to breathe different things, but they only can commit to one, and most just go with fire or lightning. Apparently her reason for this was that nobody expects acid, and is always ready to get hit with fire or lightning from a Draconian. And honestly, she's got a point.

As for myself and Micah, we went back to the planet Alia Mev-Rossar lived on to find out what more he knew. There was no way in all the realms that his house was the sole hide of his story. A guy like him? His house probably wasn't even where the most of his knowledge was kept.

When Micah and I returned to that unnamed planet, there was something new there that wasn't present before. Ghosts wandered the streets of this old world, in the ruined cities. Micah explained that the planet's orbital path was along a spatial rift, and these Psionic Spectres were manifesting as a result of the imbalance of powers and energies. One of them walked up to me and greeted me, and in that instant I realized that these people had no idea that they were dead. So I played along, asked if he knew a Cevian named Alia Mev-Rossar. He said he knew a Cevian, but not if that was his name. Micah seemed confused at first that I was so quick to act in the way I had, and even after I explained to her what I was doing, she said, "I know, I just never pegged you as one who does that."

As this spirit and I talked, he suddenly stopped in his place. He was confused, as he questioned why the city appeared to be in ruin all of a sudden. I told him that I couldn't be sorrier if I tried, but since he was now seeing me, someone from outside his vision in death, the veil was lifting.

The spirit took it far better than most might, but he still despaired, calling, "I remember now the day the heavens boiled." I asked him if he could tell me his story, to which he asked if he could just show me, so I let him.

The heavens boiled indeed on that day, when the city was under assault by raiders, who looked to take advantage of the mostly hidden location for the fact that there'd be little consequence for their actions. I saw through the eyes of the spirit as he rushed into the home of Alia Mev-Rossar and told him he had to get out of there, and the city was being evacuated. Alia insisted that he needed to hide a set of blueprints, and asked if there was anywhere that it could assuredly fall into no one's hands, especially not the wrong ones. The location of 'Legshatter Cavern' was suggested, a remote cavern a good two hundred miles (though he used the measurement of three hundred Raks) east of a remote town on a different continent. Alia said it'd work, and ran off through a hidden tunnel as the raiders entered the home. He fought valiantly, likely buying the time for Alia to escape, but after killing about twelve of them, fell to their weapons.

The vision stopped, and the spirit still had a heavy voice as he came to realize why his home was in disheveled ruin.

That's when I discovered a new power of mine with The Aura, though I didn't realize that it was so rare at the time. I looked through the veil of the past with the sight of The Aura, and traced back what once was until I reached the moment I was looking for. Having used this literal clairvoyance to see into the past in perfect detail, I turned to the spirit and told him that his city was never ruined. The invaders were fought off successfully, and Alia Mev-Rossar escaped with the blueprints for the Way Gate to the Field of Unreality because of his sacrifice, that now might save all of the universe in the now. The state of his home was simply the natural course of time, and decay. A remote planet that people gradually left or lived the rest of their lives on, and the story of this world was peaceful in the end.

The spirit thanked me, and vanished to his rest. Micah pointed out that there were still many others around still walking this yearly cycle, and that we had a job to do. I told her that we got the information we needed, plus a bonus soul laid to rest.

Her surprise was still present, she really just never thought of me like that. Pleasantly surprised, but surprised all the same. Legshatter Cavern awaited, however, in all its foreboding name might suggest.

I couldn't help but feel like Micah and I were taking our time a bit much on our trip between the two provinces on this planet, and she could tell, what with her insistence that the universe wouldn't fall in a day, and that our allies would let us know if we needed to make haste. It was helpful for her to reassure me like that as we soon found the cave, and it sure looked like it had every right to be called Legshatter Cavern. The maw that was its entrance was a jagged and awkward drop along tooth-like stalagmites that promised no easy way down.

I asked Micah if she could make this climb. With her signature wit and cheek she told me, "Are you joking? I test hands-on some of the best security in the galaxies, I could climb this piss-drunk and blindfolded."

And then she zoomed right on down like I was a fool for questioning her, and I mean, I sure was. I first thought I'd have to wait and see what she found, but then I remembered one of my Autotelekinetic Cantrips, and simply walked on down via Psionic platforms summoning themselves beneath my feet to form a staircase courtesy of The Aura. Micah asked me why I didn't do that earlier. I told her I forgot I could up until that moment, to which she nodded, and we pressed forth.

There seemed to be a small altar at the bottom of the crags, a shrine that Alia Mev-Rossar must have constructed, given that it bore the seal of Sais-Vann, an entity from the Cevian mythological pantheon, I only hesitate to say 'god of' like a singular term because Sais-Vann's domain was simultaneously safe havens, writers and sharpshooters. The first part of that equation was the purpose of the shrine here at Legshatter Cavern, the concealment of a sanctuary of knowledge. In this case, knowledge to lead to Arigen Concarius's Field of Unreality. The cavern's tunnel extended further into darkness, at the end of which we found Alia Mev-Rossar's final home and resting place.

Built of the chamber at the end of the tunnel of Legshatter Cavern, Alia Mev-Rossar had made a hidden home for himself. The undisturbed cave air preserved this abode of his for an unfathomably long time, where we found a primitive bed of stone slab frame, carved shelves of chamber's walls filled with handwritten volumes bound in scraps of cave-creature leather (usually small lizards for the area and time) that had been stitched together until large enough to form the binding. Micah wanted to take them to Xenidar and I agreed wholeheartedly. We searched the chamber, grabbing every scrap we could to analyze at The Hideout to see if the plans for the Way Gate to the Field of Unreality were among them.

On our last run between the Aura Runner and Legshatter Cavern, it started to rain, so Micah and I stayed in the cave for a bit, even though we could've easily put up an environmental shield over us to make sure we didn't get wet. It was one of those moments where we just silently agreed to take this one moment to just enjoy that strangely primal comfort of being in a cave while it poured rain outside.

Even then, I still couldn't shake the ticking clock that was The Unmaker and his campaign against the universe. The looming ever-threat that hung over me constantly as I took this little break that had me wondering how much ground we were losing by not being constantly on the move. It probably would've been a lot louder if I were still mortal.

Micah snapped me out of that thinking by bonking me on the head with a wooden stick she had been carrying, which she called 'The No Sense of Impending Doom Allowed Stick.' I asked her why she was had it. She said that she just grabbed a nice-looking stick while on the way over, and as soon as she saw me dooming up a storm in my head, decided that this was the purpose of the stick.

"Radien, the universe won't fall in a day. Not even to The Unmaker," she told me before sitting on the stone slab that was likely once Alia Mev-Rossar's bed in this cave when he lived there. I was hardly even thinking when I conjured up a mattress for her to sit on that would make it more comfortable, and she certainly didn't seem to mind.

"I know, Micah," I told her. "But I cannot ignore the pace at which The Unmaker moves, just as I cannot ignore that we have yet to be a step ahead of him in this fight."

"Believe me, I get it. But please, continue to believe me when I say that we can afford to take one night's worth of a breather."

I sat down next to her and sighed as well, unsure of what to say. It felt like the entire conversation we could've otherwise had just happened all at once in that exchange.

Hardly any point in continuing, we'd just be reiterating our points with different words until one of us got frustrated.

But there we were, just sitting next to each other and hearing the sound of the rain outside the cave, and above us on the ground. She was correct, the universe wouldn't fall in a day. But I remember that on Earth, you absolutely could. I don't think people realize just how awful that planet was when I was on it, even Humans now. How it drained you of your very soul, your sense of existence, how every design was perfectly tailored to grind you to dust over the slowest and most agonizing death possible, even if there wasn't any physical pain involved.

I just... gods dammit, I should be over that fucking planet now! It's been well over six hundred years, I've spent so much longer off that wretched rock than I did on it! If I can't get over a measly few decades, then I don't deserve the splendor of the centuries! I *order* myself to move the *fuck* on from that stupid hunk of stone!

So we eventually did finally get back to Turazin, precious cargo in tow, and it went without incident. Everyone was still there after the few days we took to find this stuff, and Xenidar began working on transcriptions immediately as I went back to the Fortress on Raon-Arashal to see how that was going. It seemed Micah was correct: the universe did not fall in a day. And thank the gods for it, because otherwise that would've been *stupid*. I don't think I could stand living in a universe where every instant is so vital like that. I still wonder how I survived those years on a planet that was precisely like that.

I was met with a very impressed-looking Veralis and Arakai, and I asked what the hell they were looking so impressed about. This was where I learned just how rare my mastery of The Aura was. My looking back through history on that ruined world to bring that wandering spirit peace, it was no small feat, as it turned out. Though scrying into the past wasn't an uncommon use of power, it often took intense and specific training to pull off in the manner I had.

Further study into just how much raw Psionic potential Humans had was sure to follow. There were no Fonts on Earth, so it was possible that the Human race would be the next Elurians as far as raw Psionic potential was concerned.

The stories were eerily similar up to a point. The Elurians came from a planet with no Fonts, a relative rarity in the universe, but were found out to be extremely Psionically inclined, and had just been terrifyingly starved throughout their whole history. The Elurians then contributed the majority of the most significant advances and developments in power-wielding, including the 'de-stylization' of the art, and subsequent destruction of the 'Psionic Meta' that had existed for a very long time.

Humans were on the brink of following in their footsteps, it seemed.

One of Alia Mev-Rossar's journals, the least ancient of them, described how he had 'deconstructed the schematics for the Way Gate and hid them across the volumes and manuals' in his hide. So grabbing everything was the right option as we scoured the texts for the blueprints hidden in plain sight. Two days in, Jarrek charged into the lab with an idea, and clearly no clue as to why he didn't think of it earlier.

# PART 2

## EXODUS TO VELANI

The oldest heraldic symbol in the universe is the Harrows of the Red Sun. It's a Redarian symbol. Well, basically it's *the* Redarian symbol. It gets its name from an artifact of the same name, a Nebula Pearl the size of a bowling ball. For reference, Nebula Pearls are usually all of a few millimeters in diameter. You could definitely make a religion from it. I mean, it's happened. Twice. But anyways, Redarian custom dictates that if the Redarian collective society falls into corruption, the Harrows is to be stolen from its resting place on Redaria Omega. In doing so, the sigil's legitimacy is preserved in a sort of 'not letting assholes ruin it' way, and it serves as a massive cultural wake-up call for all Redarians, that says things have to change. Stealing the Harrows, according to Jarrek, would snap The Unmaker's influence from the Redarians who were currently affected. By his own testimony: "The Harrows and the meaning of its theft are far more ingrained in our culture than The Unmaker could ever dream of being. We take the

Harrows, and Redaria is back in the fight," Micah concurred during this discussion, and even recommended that Jarrek be the one to actually take the Harrows. The theft of the Harrows had up to that point been done sixteen times in all of history, and never by someone who held an office of power, let alone a military one, let alone an Arch-Militant themselves. Though Micah was more qualified to execute the theft, it would be that much stronger of a message if Jarrek did it.

Granted, that conversation had no shortage of banter, and threats from Micah to bonk me with the stick she took from Alia Mev-Rossar's home planet, that now doubled as 'The Educate Radien on Basic Redarian Culture Stick.' Honestly, I suspect she was just in a bit of a bonking mood.

We soon got ahold of the public floorplan of the building that housed the Harrows on Redaria Omega, and Jarrek noted that additional surveillance cameras were installed to cover the blind spots that allowed the last theft to take place earlier within the Eighth Cosmic Era, not coincidentally shortly before the Soul-Caste was abandoned. These cameras were not on the public plans. Jarrek then produced a 'true' floorplan map of the Harrows's resting place, which apparently had gone under very few changes over its history, which was apparently part of the point. The Harrows is not the single hardest object to steal on Redaria Omega, but the Hall of Heroes in the city of Fassorat it was housed in was no slouch. Micah also pointed out that the non-impossibility of the task is part of the point.

It became clear as well that as much as The Unmaker definitely thought about the Harrows, and the possibility that someone would symbolically steal it as custom demanded, there wasn't really anything he could do about it. The Harrows was much older than The Unmaker, and the meaning of its theft was more a part of Redarian culture than he could ever achieve. This supported the theory that stealing the Harrows would break The Unmaker's grip on the Redarians of the Velani Array, and likely by effect, the entire solar system itself just for the fact that everyone knew just what it meant when the Harrows was stolen.

I asked Jarrek how the hell he got access to all the information he had on the Hall of Heroes despite The Unmaker. He reminded me that he was still the Arch-Militant, and he couldn't be stripped of his rank unless all of the branches of the Militarium agreed to do so. And since Nathineyl had not fallen, Nathineyl was what made sure that the motion never passed. So he still had all the rights and privileges of his commission as Arch-Militant, and could order that he be given the true floorplan of the Hall of Heroes.

Even with the additional cameras, Micah still was able to devise a route for Jarrek to get in and out of the vault that held the Harrows, we'd just have to be his eyes on the outside of the building as he snuck his way in.

At that moment, Xenidar walked into the room and told us that he had something that would help Micah and myself out once we got to Redaria Omega.

It was a pair of Morphic Illusion Generators that Ellan had grabbed during his last cavalry raid of the SWEEPS base, and local tech sensors wouldn't pick them up because they weren't of any known make. I realized then that this was

Human technology. Being out and about in the universe, the Humans had gotten to the point where they were making their own advanced techpieces, and the Human 'style' of their looks and creation was only just being ironed out. It made for a perfectly smuggleable Morphic Illusion Generator, in this case. It would also be able to hide our Talismans while we were there. Jarrek wouldn't need one, because he was supposed to be the one to steal the Harrows. But Micah and I would be disguised while on Redaria Omega. Xenidar had patched the software to be able to make a convincing Redarian morph, and when I turned it on, a shimmer passed over me and I looked down to see that indeed, I looked like a Redarian now.

Of course, the form being a holographic projection just over my skin, I didn't actually feel like I took the form. More like I was wearing a half-assed suit that didn't really click like your good one might. I commented that I wished I could actually feel the tail, and Micah reminded me that Jaden and the GAMA were an option. I still had to narrow my choice from five remaining, Redarian admittedly one of the candidates.

Getting on Redaria Omega, and to the Hall of Heroes was the easy part. The hard part was in Jarrek's hands once he looked at the wall he was planning to scale in order to make his entrance.

"You got this, Jarrek?" I asked him.

"Of course I do. You think I became Arch-Militant by hiding behind a desk and playing Office Vulture? No, I lead from the front."

He's a clever one, that Jarrek. And so Micah and I were left to make sure our exit route was clear, as well as that no one snuck up on us during the heist. As we scouted our route together, a Redarian came up to us with the first half of a phrase.

"For eight days he slaved at the forge, to forge the slave that could open the Eye."

I replied. "But the Eye was shut to slave and slaver, for its sight could pierce the veil of their scheme."

It was an excerpt from a book called *The Eye of Akoraveon,* that recounted the known tale of an Archaeotech artifact by the same name. I had read the book during some of my downtime.

The Redarian before us saluted with the Redarian salute, and not The Unmaker's, then showing his Talisman around his wrist instead of his neck. Bit riskier, but more concealable. So we showed him ours, decloaking them for a brief moment.

He at first tried to inform us that the resistance in Fassorat was already making plans to steal the Harrows, but when Micah asked if those plans involved Arch-Militant Wöllschlager being the one to actually take the Harrows, he admitted that was a much better plan than what they had. I asked him if he could clear us an escape route, and he was already head of us, instructing two of his operatives to aid in the scouting.

At the time, we didn't know how long it would take for the theft of the Harrows to work, if it even was going to. Micah pulled up on a screen the live public feed of the

Harrows in its resting chambers, and we waited for Jarrek to make his entry.

Sparks flew as something cut through a ventilation duct in the chamber, and a hole was kicked out. From it jumped down a Redarian with a claymore on his back that was about his own height.

"My name is Jarrek Wöllschlager, I am the Arch-Militant of the Redarian Interplanetary Battlefleet, and I am taking possession of the Harrows of the Red Sun."

He then grabbed the bowling-ball sized Nebula Pearl and put it in a protective briefcase. Jarrek then unslung the claymore from his back and replaced it with the case, his weapon in his hands and his cargo strapped to his shoulders as the Honor Guard burst through the door.

It was standoffish, at first, and Jarrek looked at them expectantly. And soon we found out that not only did the plan work, it worked fast. Jarrek grabbed the comm-link from one of the now-free Honor Guards, and tuned it to a specific frequency only he had access to.

"Initiate emergency activation of the Velani Dyson Swarm, shield configuration. Authorization voice key Arch-Militant Wöllschlager, three-six-two-one, Kandor-Hex."

Micah seemed surprised at this, commenting. "Wait, we finished the Dyson Swarm?"

I could only say "Wait, you guys have a Dyson Swarm?!"

But the effect was clear. The theft of the Harrows had done exactly what we needed it to, and the Velani Array was now back in the fight against The Unmaker. Jarrek and the

Honor Guard from the Hall of Heroes stepped out with their heads held high, and one for the history books. About halfway down the steps outside the building's entrance, Jarrek stopped in his tracks as he realized something.

"Wait, fuck, I forgot to put it back." He then spun around to run back into the Hall to return the Harrows to its chamber.

About a day later, we saw the shimmer of the shield's activation planetside. A few tweaks to the shield's frequency, and now The Unmaker's telepathic subterfuge couldn't get through, nor any hostile ship.

So now I had time to try to figure out more of the code that was the hidden blueprints for the Way Gate to the Field of Unreality. Then I remembered that Alia Mev-Rossar's field of study was Phase-Engineering, not Cryptology. There was no damn code, and he meant exactly what he said when he deconstructed the schematics for the Way Gate and hid them across the volumes and manuals. The fragments of the schematics themselves were physically among the pages, disguised as parts of their books. Drawings were incorporated into doodles of random theory, bit by bit obfuscating the true nature of the whole.

Within a month, I had the plans for the Way Gate. Every brick was accounted for, and that was much more important than one might realize at first.

The Way Gate was made with Rune Bricks. An old but not obsolete form of Psionic power generation that allows for extremely specific frequencies and wavelengths to be achieved by fusing tailored kinds of power to each individual brick. The reason it's not considered obsolete is because it's extremely reliable and the ultimate safe bet when designing a complex system like a Way Gate straight out of the universe itself. It wouldn't be impossible to redesign to more modern and compact specifications, but I had neither the patience to make that conversion, nor the willingness to risk it not working. Rune Bricks were exactly what you used when you didn't want to risk it not working, and that's precisely what I had here.

Only problem was that there were five hundred eighty-six individually crafted bricks in the circle alone that made up the platform, and that's not counting the binding mundane runes around the bricks on the base, and the two intersecting arches that went above it. I sure as hell had my work cut out for me, and thank the gods Jarrek got the Dyson Swarm up and running around the Velani Array, or I might not have the time.

Wait, scratch that, five hundred eighty-nine. The centermost part of the circle was made up of four bricks that were each half the size of a standard one.

The actual runework on these bricks were well-documented, the only hassle there was with compiling all the information on scribing them all was the fact that it was so rare for Rune Brick structures to have different inscriptions for each brick. Normally at most it was four or five different energetic sigils, just done over and over again in a pattern. But when you wanted something that specific and controlled, it wasn't out of the question.

It's not far from saying, "One, two, three, four, five,

six, seven, eight, nine, ten" instead of just "One through ten."

So there I was, carving all these individual bricks with meticulousness and scrutiny to detail, knowing full well that I couldn't start getting impatient with them to the point where I wanted to rush. There were days where I got twenty bricks made. Others where I barely got halfway done with one. But I still knew that I needed to be able to devote energy to this like it was a fresh day one every time, and that if I had to take that much time, I had to take that much time.

But even with the Velani Dyson Swarm providing a shield both from The Unmaker himself and his goons, I still was looking over my shoulder at almost every moment, checking in with Jarrek as his fleet patrolled the system. He even told me a few times that vigilance wasn't my job at the moment. Right as he was... I still could not ignore the very real threat of the zealots of The Unmaker.

Zealots, thralls, minions, devotees, acolytes, pawns, cultists... why do I know so many words for enemies, yet not a single one to mean more than friend or ally? That... shattering word eludes me, yet I can rattle off so many others that call someone my foe. It's fine though, to be perfectly honest. Friends and allies are more than I thought I'd ever get in my life. So I'm glad to have the ones that I can call such now.

Unfortunately, the Rune Bricks were a tedious process, especially with the way I was doing it, making sure it was done right. But as long as I at least chiseled something, anything, a single symbol upon one brick, that was a non-zero amount of progress. And there was a finite number of bricks I needed to do, so every step forward was very much that. I even configured another Autotelekinetic Cantrip with The Aura; summoning a literal progress bar for each brick and the overall construction. Being able to see that physically tick up was a great help. With each stroke and each symbol, now I no longer had to rely solely on just telling myself I was moving forward. I could see it too. And that's what I needed. I needed to be able to see it.

Gods, *there's* what I was fucking missing on Earth. Being able to believe I was actually progressing towards something. A green bar that only I could see did more for me in three seconds than the four therapists my parents had forced me to go to during my life on Earth could dream of in their most power-tripping, egotistical nights, combined. But we are not here to discuss that, Effigy. We are here for me to tell you the story of how I got here, now, with you, this one last time.

Jaden offered to send me a few of her assistants to help with the Rune Bricks, and I told her that if they had the skill and the willingness, they were more than welcome to do as much as they wished. We were setting up the Way Gate on one of Redaria Omega's two moons, Aldin. We rejected Virak from the plan because Aldin's forests are way better, and forests are badass places to set up mystical Psionic structures near or within. So given that we were that close to Laksor, Jaden's detachment got here within the day to start helping me out.

Our progress remained slow but steady and sure. I decided to take a break from my direct involvement to regain my spirit and zeal on the matter of creating all these Rune

Bricks. Well, I say 'decided,' but it was more of an insistence from Micah, and the fact that she'd likely bug me to take a break until I did. The energy it would've taken to fend off her legitimate arguments coupled with simply crafting the bricks... yeah, it was the logical choice.

Unfortunately, this meant I had some time to ponder about the situation we were all in. The Dyson Swarm's shield made sure that there was no easy way into the solar system, and I also realized that none of The Unmaker's actions were actually outright destructive. Physically speaking, at least. Sure, he was supplanting everyone's memories, but despite this, he had destroyed no cities, and killed no people. Those that died were his followers that we had killed in our resistance. But their blood is equally on his hands, as he was the one who had to force their hypnotized bodies into situations where they would be destroyed, namely, trying to take us prisoner and convert us.

So it was honestly entirely possible that the Dyson Shield had given us just... a permanent sanctuary. Sure, more hostile action would be taken against us as soon as we threatened to incur where he was in the Field of Unreality, but until then... We honestly had all the time we wanted. The Dyson Shield was still a Dyson Swarm, and was harnessing all the energy that the Velani star was outputting. We could just stay here. The Velani Array is three single planets, a binary system, and dozens of moons around the solid and gas giant planets here. No shortage of space. I could just have all my adventures and my explorations here.

Hell, I even knew that The Unmaker *had* to have a

reason for wanting everyone to call him the hero, even if I didn't know what that reason was. And maybe he might die of old age eventually, or exhaustion from keeping everyone his puppet. Then the whole thing would've blown over and all we had to do was wait...

I can't describe the prospect as tempting, because I didn't find myself actively tempted in either direction. Viable, sure, but I could see myself in the future as I looked forward into it. Staring longingly and contemplatively at the barrier of the Dyson Shield for countless hours, debating with myself whether it was time or not to see, wondering if I had made the right choice in staying...

For all the space and splendor a cage the size of a solar system might contain, it would still be at the end of the day, a cage all the same. And I'd still find myself looking beyond the bars, wondering and fantasizing. And who would I be if I chose to rest on such low laurels? Not me, I know that.

Even during the break Micah had downright ordered me to take, I found myself along that edge in the Aura Runner, staring at the shield that separated the Velani Array from a universe of The Unmaker's design. I don't know why it felt so calm to me. I knew that just beyond that shield was likely a trap around every corner, and behind it was the constant effort to disarm them all. And yet I found calmness at the edge of the storm like it was the eye instead.

The communications panel of the Aura Runner's cockpit pinged. Apparently, Veralis's ship, the Celestial Dart, was not too far away. A message popped up onscreen.

*YOU KNOW, PATROLLING THE DYSON SHIELD DOESN'T*

*REALLY COUNT AS A BREAK.*

I sighed as I opened the channel.

"What do you want?" I asked, and she raised an eyebrow to my tone. "Sorry, I just... did you need something?"

She asked to come aboard for a quick visit, and I didn't see anything wrong with letting her beam on. It was at that moment I realized I'd never actually showed her the inside of the Aura Runner. She took a look around, and nodded.

"It's definitely the kind of ship you'd have," she commented, and I couldn't help but chuckle in agreement.

"But did you need something?" I reiterated my question.

To this, she just kind of... looked at me like she was trying to read me. As soon as I saw one of her eyes flash amber, I immediately shot up from my chair, steeled and ready. I projected the image in my mind of dozens of gates slamming shut as the intruder was yanked away from seeing what lied within.

There was a strange kind of shock on her face as I just stood there, unflinching and unfazed.

"I'm sorry," she said. "I didn't know you took it that seriously."

I nodded slowly before speaking. "My mind is my own, Veralis. I will not have it read."

"You know, my Psionic Empathy is about as much reading one's mind as reading body language. A surface-level observation that I still have to draw a conclusion from."

"I see."

She then sat down on one of the nearby seats along the wall. The actual cockpit section of the Aura Runner ran along most of the hull's length, as it was the cargo bay that had that pocket dimension, bigger-on-the-inside type of technology. As much as I'd bet I could configure the bridge to be like that as well, I never actually did it. I never felt the need to have that much space here on it.

"But I do get it," Veralis said. "I do understand how *any* sort of ability like mine could be seen as straight-up mind-reading. Which by the way, I do agree that it's a total dick move. Outright mind-reading, that is."

She still had yet to tell me if she needed anything, so I asked one more time.

"No, I don't," Veralis finally answered. "And I don't want to say that I wanted to check in with you, because not only is that untrue, I also bet you'd hate that reason."

I nodded. I always have found it extremely annoying when people did that, checking in. If you claim to be my friend, then why would you have such a lack of trust in my own self-stability that you feel the need to constantly verify it for yourself? Such unjustified and patronizing borderline coddling is not the action of a friend, but a manipulator, in my experience. That said, it was at least the case that Veralis's reason for her visit wasn't that.

"To be honest, I've been doing the same thing you have on my off days," she finally explained. "Figured we might as well meet up in our mutual downtime, see if that makes it pass any more comfortably."

She leaned forward in her seat with a sigh, putting her

forearms on her thighs as I saw her ears flatten with annoyance at this whole Unmaker situation. It was admittedly not a side of her I'd ever seen before, but I also knew well that I didn't know everything there was to know about Veralis Stratenheim, so I wasn't going to act shocked.

I soon found myself sitting across from her on the seats on the other side of that wall, in a similar position as she righted herself and leaned back a little.

"Yeah, I get it," I said plainly, because I did get it. I did definitely relate to that sort of fatigued relaxing, where in your relaxing, you end up showing how fatigued you are. Her ears perked up as she looked towards me once I commented that. "Hell, The Aura makes it so that I don't have to sleep. It boosts my stamina so that I don't feel tired. It enhances my mental acuity so that I don't get exhausted... right? So why then, I wonder, do I find myself looking so fatigued when no one's looking?"

Veralis just listened as I debated internally whether or not to say the next sentence of that thought. It didn't come out easily. I still wonder if it was wise to let it.

"Moreover, I wonder why I find myself willing to look it around another."

"Probably because I just did a few moments ago," Veralis enlightened. "You know you're not the only one feeling it, and that you wouldn't be the only person in the room to have shown it."

I nodded. That made sense. I did say that as well. "That does make sense, aye."

"As for fatigue..." Veralis said, standing up briefly to

then sit next to me, which came as a surprise, to be perfectly honest. "The Aura allows you to understand pretty much every language out there. That includes your own body's."

I looked over to her briefly, and found myself fighting the temptation to pet her on the head. I mean, I didn't know what the customs for headpats were among the species, so many of them having fur and all. As much as Veralis's ears looked quite soft and rubbable, I didn't want to accidentally find myself committing a social faux pas on the level of... well, interpret as you will.

Not to mention seeing this six-foot-two Cynofrax Vulpian sitting right next to me so casually, I had to work pretty hard to remain as casual in demeanor as normal. I never have been used to someone actually sitting *next* to me by deliberate choice, let alone someone a full eight inches taller than me.

That was the thing, she got up from her seat across from me and switched to that one, and my mind's gears were spinning like crazy for it.

"Normally, your stomach might growl and you've no idea what you want to eat. But with The Aura, you do. Maybe you can even tell that it's because you're bored, rather than actually hungry." Veralis continued. "And with fatigue, that's The Aura telling you to take a damn break. Believe me, Radien, you're not the only person who's getting nagged by the lifeblood of the universe itself to take a day off."

"Fair enough," I added. "Thanks."

I then remembered when the last time was we were sitting next to each other like this. It was just after the Planet of Traitors had happened, and I had just made the case to Cynofrax's conclave to disgrace the Exiled Chapter Vulpians from the annals of the species, and rename the planet thusly. I wondered very hard if I should share that. My instincts told me not to, and my mind did the same. Unfortunately, my instincts told me that it also might not be a bad idea, and my mind was making the point that Veralis had already shown her fatigue and shared what she had with me already.

So basically, both of the things that make my decisions were in direct conflict with each other. But I also could not ignore that Veralis was not a human. She was Vulpian. Cynofrax Vulpian, and that's a hell of a lot better.

"I remember the last time we were sitting like this," I started.

"You barely were resting your head on my shoulder for all of a minute before you went off to the Font near Rahkess Forest." Veralis chuckled. "Your whole upper body was tense as a rock. Kinda defeated the purpose, I thought."

This truly surprised me. Not the fact she also was thinking about it, but *that* is what she remembered from that day? Not the conversation before, or the things I said during it? Things that I still stand beside, that I still expect to be held to for saying them.

"That's the first thing you remember of it?" I couldn't help but say. "Not the things I said, or the—"

"Yup," she cut off. "That is correct."

I didn't know what to say from there. Hell, I had a whole defense prepared for if she started that conversation again, counterpoints and arguments in case she tried to sell me some kind of 'share the load' bullshit. But she didn't. That was what surprised me most of all.

At least, that *was* the most surprising thing for all of a few seconds before I felt Veralis grab my hand and place it atop her head near her ears, and in a sort of 'autopilot,' I found myself giving her those headpats and earrubs I had been so tempted to earlier. After a few moments of this sort of 'automatic fuzzy-rubbing protocol engaged' from me (which definitely had been ingrained from the cats I'd taken care of in my youth), Veralis laid back along the row of chairs, stretching out a bit as her head leaned rested against my thigh, and I transitioned into cheek rubs. My own cheeks were likely bright red by then.

Even in this space with you, Effigy, where I know no others can listen, I still find it embarrassing as hell to say that Veralis's fur is actually *really nice and soft*. She must take good care of it.

I noticed that her eyes were closed after a bit, so I assumed she had fallen asleep, and I could stand back up and let her rest. But then she suddenly started lightly chewing on my hand for ceasing the pets, so with red still on my face, I had no choice but to continue.

After a bit, with her hands folded across her belly, she asked me, "Radien, how do I ask you a personal question?"

I told her the truth. "By saying the words, and understanding that I will give a truthful answer."

"When the Way Gate is finished, when the time to take down The Unmaker is nigh, are you planning to go alone?"

"If that's what I have to do, then I will do that."

"We both know that's not the whole answer."

With a sigh, I said the rest of my piece. "I told you that I would give you a truthful answer. That doesn't mean I'm an open book."

Veralis sat back up and looked at me as she awaited the final part of that statement.

"I hope it doesn't come down to that, though," I told her. "I'd rather not find myself having to do that."

After we parted ways, I remained in my ship for another hour before heading back towards civilization. While on course for Aldin, the moon we were building the Way Gate on, The Aura Runner's sensors picked up what appeared to be a derelict space station. I found it odd, as this place did not appear on any records of past and present space stations in the Velani Array. Knowing that I was still on my Micah-mandated break, I decided to head over.

All the while as I approached, I felt an odd sensation that something was shifting. Or rather, that something *had* shifted. And not with The Unmaker or anything like that, no... something deeper. As if the air itself had suddenly changed... alignment, for lack of a better word.

If you saw dust particles floating in the air, and then they all suddenly shifted a few inches to the left unprompted and then continued falling, you wouldn't feel any sensation on your skin, or change in the nonexistent wind. But you'd have seen all the dust, in unison, shift.

It was like that. As if something very fundamental had just changed. Not broken, not knocked out of place... just...

changed. It was unnerving as hell, and now I knew I had to keep going, or it'd never stop bothering me.

The station was devoid of atmosphere, so I put my Personal Defense Grid Generator on my belt to give me an oxygen shield. With passive cantrips from The Aura keeping me grounded with as close to a 'personal gravity alignment' as I could get, I entered the ghost station.

The halls were as barren as I expected, and the unnerving feeling of the winds beneath the wind remained. I'm not sure if I was overcome with dread or not, because I felt like the sensation of dread was passing through me, in all but the emotion itself. The harrowing harmonic hum that grew louder and louder as if my head were an echo chamber, the feeling as though my hands traveled through sand that offered no resistance. The surreal lack of any idea just what the hell I was feeling or noticing, like my eyes could see forever in a plane of nothingness.

"What in all the realms is happening to me?" I said aloud, if only to break the silence.

I turned around to meet a presence I felt, and saw a silvery figure that seemed to barely exist in the third dimension with the texture of a sheet of melted bismuth.

"Time Ender," I realized.

Somehow I understood that this was the same one I encountered on Homphalion, just before another such spell of surreality. All the same feelings added up. It was all there last time, too.

I stood there and waited for his declaration, or whatever it was that awaited me from the creature.

"Well, what are you waiting for?" I challenged him. Or them, hell if I had any clue.

"The Unmaker has enthralled one of my kinsmen, and his power over linear time belongs to the destroyer of history." The Time Ender said, but not in the hoarse voice that brought tidings of doom back on Homphalion. No, this voice was urgent and had no time for theatrics. "This cannot continue."

"I remember what you did on Homphalion. You created some kind of chrono-anchor, a checkpoint in time. I did something irredeemable later, and suddenly found myself back at the start, like I reloaded the save after I fucked up," I told him, trying to comprehend to any capacity just what the hell the purpose of these guys was.

"Neither myself or my people experience time as a linear course of cause and effect, and rarely do we elect to partake in the course itself. But the words you choose, they are indeed what you experienced when last we encountered."

Figures that there's a beyond-time species in the universe. Had to be somewhere, and thank the gods they weren't malevolent. Assuming these guys weren't gods in their own right. But I could see where the conversation was going. With a Time Ender lending his power to The Unmaker, he could practice breaching the Dyson Shield as many times as he damn well pleased, unless the scales could be balanced. I told him that little epiphany of mine, and I could sense solemnity from the Time Ender, even if there was no real way for his physical form to convey it.

"I'll give you the benefit of assuming you know what

you're doing, since you're the one who lives outside of linear time and all. What do I do about this wayward Time Ender?"

"Five days from now, an attack will occur on the single weakest point of the Dyson Shield. It will be broken through within a matter of minutes, and not a single missile more than necessary will be used. From there, they will enter the solar system itself, and transmit The Unmaker's message on all frequencies," the Ender began to explain.

"The communications frequencies have been shuffled and secured," I informed him. "They'd have to transmit directly from one of the towers planetside."

"Not if they knew the precise frequency," he corrected. "And they've only rehearsed this as many times as one would need to simply try them all."

This was damned frustrating. True, but annoying as all hell. So what the hell was I to do, I asked him.

"To kill my former kinsmen is to sever the connection they have to their anchor. Once that is done, upon your return to this time and place, the attack will have been prevented, as his influence through time is erased. No, this will not affect what he has already done within the past or present, as it is merely the end of his personal span. The events in your future he has affected are a part of his past, and–"

"I get it," I swiftly cut him off. "So the save point for me is here and now."

"As one might say, yes."

I told him to keep a close eye on me whenever I was outside the Dyson Shield, and if I was beginning to slip into The Unmaker's control, or be about to die, to return me to the checkpoint Chrono-Anchor. He agreed. I had five days to make this happen, and with the help of the Time Ender, as many tries as I needed.

And so began my first run. The Aura Runner exited the Dyson Sphere with a quick phase-jump, and I set course for the hideout of the Time Ender, which my friendly one said was on a planet called Ultharn. The travel time alone would take two days if I was to remain undetected, or an hour if I was full speed ahead. Since it was the first run, I took the two-day route. And sure enough, two days later, Ultharn was in view. But holy hell, was it a fortress. While still out of the planet's detection range, I did a Deep-Field scan-pulse on the whole thing. That was another whole day.

So the thing about scans, there's basically three main types. Regular, Wide-Field, and Deep-Field. A regular one can give you the elemental composition and readout of a planet in all of a few minutes. But that's just atoms. Planets are more than atoms, they're chemicals and structures and compounds and such. A Wide-Field scan-pulse can rectify the absence of compound relevancy that a regular one has. That one... on a planet Ultharn's size, two hours at most. Depends mostly on the processing power of the scanner.

A Deep-Field pulse, however, does one extra. It's the scan that reasons rather than simply thinks. A Wide-Field pulse could notice that there's a big underground area with a high concentration of silicon, cobalt, gold, silver, copper, steel, aluminum, and such. But the Deep-Field pulse is what actually figures out that it's a big underground server room.

A regular scan can tell you that something is there. A

Wide-Field scan can tell you *what* is there. A Deep-Field scan can tell you *why* it's there. With a slight margin of error, but hardly anyone bothers with Deep-Field pulses anyway. It's a much longer process, takes a lot more power, and doesn't actually typically make a big difference if you can just put two and two together yourself.

But this was the run to learn. These five days I had were the ones I'd be using to just get information.

So on day three of five for run one, I now had a clue what I was dealing with. Ultharn's fortifications had been built specifically to protect the Time Ender, who was hiding out not far from the core of the planet, behind an armada in orbit, billions of soldiers on the ground, innumerable maze-like underground tunnels, and only the most elaborately secure vault in the damn universe.

Knowing full well I had as many tries as I needed, I looked at the weapons the Aura Runner possessed. I admittedly had never needed to consider using them up until then. The front-mounted pair of twin-linked Ion Cannons likely wouldn't do anything themselves, let alone the top and bottom defensive auto-lasers. But the payload weapons the ship had, listed as "Pulsar Missiles," could probably do something impressive.

So with that knowledge, I fired off one of the missiles. It punched a sizable hole in the shield that surrounded the planet, to my surprise. Soon, the Aura Runner was surrounded by the armada that guarded the planet, and I called out to the empty air "Shit, reload, reload!" as a desperate plea to the Time Ender, which he thankfully understood, as I found myself standing in the seemingly derelict station once again.

"A bold move, but unwise," he commented.

"Gimme a break, I'd never used my ship's missiles before," I told him, panting as I sure as hell felt like I just got yanked back through time, to correct my error in tactics. I couldn't tell if he actually nodded in physical space, but it sure seemed like it did.

So I did that two-day warp again, having in my memory the results of the Deep-Field scan-pulse, so I didn't have to spend another day doing the scan again.

That's another thing I found out about my pseudo-eidetic memory, and of time itself in a way. I still had experienced those days, those hours, and I could recall them and the images my eyes saw, even though they had been effectively erased as far as linear time was concerned. The Aura allowed me to see with perfect clarity my prior memories, and among them was the results of that scan-pulse.

With three days left instead of two, I had the information I possessed once before about Ultharn.

I sat in my ship, staring at the damned bastion of a planet, drawing metaphor after metaphor that I despised before finally trying to figure out how to warp-in down to the surface without setting off all the alarms they undoubtedly had.

The reason I gave Ellan a Tesla Key back on Turazin was because I had a better one on board the Aura Runner. So with my Tesla Key, I started analyzing all their frequencies, looking for the one that was tied to their phase sensors.

It took a whole day, but I did find out how to safely jump past the orbital blockade and get about a mile underground. Any further, and I'd risk teleporting into solid rock. Not a very healthy idea.

The next two days were spent hugging the left wall, turning at every turn and treating it like the maze it was as that recallable memory of mine logged the inner workings of the subterranean... well, I can't really bring myself to say labyrinth because labyrinths only have one route, by definition. I just really didn't want to say 'maze' twice in a row.

And so I kept at it, spending two days to get there silently, dropping in undetected, and then the next three tracing the route. I don't want to count how many times it took to do. I don't want to remember how long I fucking spent dealing with that bastard maze.

And after this deliberately indeterminate number of days and tries, I finally had a route to the Time Ender in his containment vault. And as soon as I saw the door, fifty feet high and five feet thick, made purely of Archonium, an alloy highly resistant to powers like The Aura, I yelled and punched a hole in the nearby wall as I told my Time Ender to pull me out. I stormed out of the station and onto my ship, pedal to the metal as I went full-throttle and full noise to Ultharn, bringing with me a modification to the Pulsar Missile loaded immediately after the one that was armed and ready.

As soon as I arrived, the armies of The Unmaker in hot pursuit, I fired off the first to break through the walls. And the second, modified one was next. The command console on my ship didn't have any big red buttons, but I would've slammed it with my fist if there were to blow that fucking planet up. That was the modification I made. A few tweaks to the payload and I had a planet killer.

Under normal circumstances, it's completely illegal in all civilized galaxies for a single ship to have planet-scale weapons of mass destruction. But these weren't normal circumstances, and the galaxies weren't civilized anymore under The Unmaker.

Ultharn crunched and collapsed from the molecular destabilization my missile brought it, and I suddenly was back at the station, facing the Time Ender who was lending me his powers. My mission was finished. The enemy Time Ender was destroyed. And the one on my side had already replaced himself into his timeline, and Ultharn was back in one piece without the bugger resting at its core.

"If I never see you again until the end of entropy, it'll be too soon," I found myself saying, angrier than I could understand why.

"I envy your frustration. I would rather do the centuries in the right order, myself," the Time Ender said, his form destabilizing and falling apart just like it did on Homphalion.

As soon as I left the station in the Aura Runner, I looked back and saw that the station had vanished. I remember distinctly that I punched the nearby wall once, but I still could not understand why, even as I did it.

I managed to get over it by the time I had a quick nap on the Aura Runner and returned to Aldin. Jaden's team had by this point created a little over an eighth of the Rune Bricks needed for the Way Gate, putting us on schedule. I made a point to not actually start laying any of the bricks until they were all finished, as the construction of the Way Gate would likely draw The Unmaker's attention, and with it, the military might of the universe under his yoke.

Unfortunately, Rune Bricks aren't quickly placed, just as they aren't quickly made. You might thing you could just use telekinesis to arrange them all, but they're surprisingly resistant to Psionic power. Naturally, they're a favorite when building fortifications. I could at best lift two at a time and place them, which would take more strain on me than if I just laid eight by hand instead. Hardly any less time, too.

I soon adopted a new routine to avoid getting pestered to take breaks by incurring Redarians named Micah, who were looking out for me to an exceptionally annoying degree. A few days spent on bricks, and a few patrolling around the edge of the Dyson Shield, seeing if there were any scouts of The Unmaker probing for weaknesses.

Of course, I never told anyone that's what I was doing on the days I wasn't making the Rune Bricks. I was telling them I was taking a break to aimlessly bugger about in space. As much as patrolling the Dyson Shield was a break as far as I was concerned, I also understood that the rest of my friends probably wouldn't see it that way.

Odd... with anyone else, I'd have taken a lot more offense to the fact that they'd insist on me taking a break. I'd meet that knowledge with a lot more hostility, a lot more hateful words at 'the insipid irrationality of people who try to claim they know you better than you know yourself.' Once again, it's probably solely because they're not Human. And I associate such controlling tendencies with Humans, since it's in their nature and all...

I guess it was really nice to hear voices other than the bastards when I first met them. It really allowed me to meet them for the first time properly, since with Humans... I always knew the patterns. If they use this phrase, they're instantly recognized as that kind of person. If they did that little motion, I immediately realize they're this other breed of shitty.

And as much as I hated to constantly hold any Human I met with an expectation of causticness and dishonor, the Humans just couldn't stop proving me right to do so.

I think I've said it at some point already, but sometimes, I really wouldn't mind being wrong.

My vigilance at the Dyson Shield was far from without benefit. I noticed ships almost daily at the edge, sniffing and scanning about for where the weak points might be, and my presence alone would shake them off.

But I never saw the same ship twice. That was quite honestly the most disturbing part. I... could easily make another joke about the nature and frequency of human toxicity, but I won't.

Wait.

Dammit.

Oh well. I've still yet to be wrong.

Regardless, my vigilance's bounty was more than usual on one day, when the Aura Runner detected a spatial anomaly.

Now then, spatial anomalies aren't uncommon on their own, but this one was one of the hard-hitters. Initial scans suggested an interdimensional gateway. Something had sent two points in space-time so out of flux that they ended up connecting to each other by way of being similarly out of flux. Again, not rare, but with The Unmaker out and about, this demanded my attention. Especially since a ship came careening out of the wormhole.

The Aura Runner quickly phase-jumped outside of the Dyson Shield, and ensnared the craft in a tractor beam, per my command, before jumping back within its safe confines. My hailing of the ship was almost simultaneous with its hailing of me.

When the visual link opened, I saw what appeared to be a cybernetically-enhanced Kanikai with blue headhair. This literally husky-looking guy clearly had a story behind him, no doubt.

"Why did you just tractor beam my ship?!" He demanded to know.

"Didn't have time to tell you why now's a really bad time to be an interdimensional traveler," I quickly answered. "I'm sure you're aware of what just happened?"

"Of course! It was *not* supposed to happen, though! There I was, working on your standard-issue potion of spatial instability, and my servo-sphere knocks over a beaker because his kinesthetic sensors are on low battery, and—"

"Right, I get it," I interrupted. Normally, I despise interrupting as much as I despise being interrupted myself. But these were not days like any other. "Look, admittedly this is just not a good time to be a visitor from another universe. Someone called The Unmaker is rewriting history with a frankly disturbing effectiveness, and we're doing all we can to find him and put him down. Your ship, the... Dropship *Snap*, was outside of where we know to be a protected area."

He took a second to process that, before imploring me to tell him more. And so I gave him the lowdown on the past years as the universe fought against The Unmaker, what had happened, what we were doing now, and the gradual inevitability of our successful defense.

Thankfully, Zevarius understood my quick actions once I explained and justified them. That was his name, by the way, Zevarius. He admittedly wasn't called Kanikai in his universe, but one of my Kanikai friends wasn't used to being called a fellow... I don't even remember the actual species name Zevarius used. Either way, it was admittedly quite amusing to see his excitement when talking to a... well, kinsmen from another universe. I'd say 'brother from another mother,' but the problem is that my experience with mothers is not good, and I'd rather not insult him with that kind of association.

Anyways, dogs never change, as it were, and Zevarius could probably bruise someone with his tail wagging as he chatted up one of our Kanikai techs at the lab.

After the tour of the facility on Aldin moon, Zevarius informed me of the necessity for him to get back to his universe, to which I concurred. I asked if he could recreate the circumstances that brought him here, but after listening to five minutes of engineering, alchemical *and* atomic mumbo-jumbo that I somehow actually understood, it was determined that the event itself was random, and we needed a controlled passage. No telling where he'd end up if he recreated the situation.

There was no shortage of glares that he shot at the hovering assistant sphere as he explained himself to this end. Granted, it was the sort of comically exaggerated glares that you give your friend when they say something as incredibly stupid as it is clever.

"Do not worry about him," Zevarius assured me. "The two of us have pulled through worse." He said as he studied the Rune Bricks that were to be used in the construction of the Way Gate to the Field of Unreality.

"He certainly seems like a good helper," I said, placing my hand on the sphere and giving a few reassuring strokes, to what I could best describe as 'happy beeps.' I really can't go into more detail what they sounded like, but believe me, you'd know happy beeps when you heard them.

"Well, after the war I fought within was over, I had nothing but time," Zevarius explained. "So, I constructed this little ball of helpfulness, and honed my skills at mechanics and cybernetics. It took a fair amount of time, not to mention countless failures, but I did eventually make him work! I have no doubt trusted him with my life on more than one occasion, just as he has put his continued existence in my hands a fair few times."

"Sounds like a hell of a story, one you'll have to tell me sometime," I commented, continuing to pat the sphere. Believe me, it worked.

"Perhaps one day, when this Unmaker of yours is not

so... all over the place," Zevarius answered, setting down the Rune Brick he was examining. "What method are you using right now to make these things?"

"Veldenite-tipped chisels to impart the energetic charge," I said, handing him one of the tools. He examined it, then asked me why we hadn't just made Veldenite stamps to simply smack onto the bricks to make it easier. I informed him that it was because that would likely break the bricks since these weren't exactly metal ingots that could be stamped upon. Not only that, but the Veldenite crystal material itself was... finicky, to put it lightly. Nobody had figured out a reliable way to make it easier.

But it definitely looked like Zevarius had an idea on how to make it work, so I let him have one of the blank bricks, and one of the chisels to experiment with, just in case he was on to something.

Of course, we had yet to address the elephant in the room, which was how exactly he was planning to get back to his reality. He admitted that he didn't really have a clue, and was more or less waiting on his mind to generate one. It's a fair method. Eventually, I took the Aura Runner over to the site from which his ship was thrown from, and saw precisely what I had suspected. Demons had figured out the existence of this new rift, and were trying to pour through. Trying, but failing. Because despite the fact that The Unmaker had control over the armies of most of the universe, it also meant that he had that much power against anyone from outside it trying to come in.

This also confirmed my suspicion that The Unmaker

wasn't a Demon. What he *was*, however, remained a mystery that I wouldn't solve until I stood face-to-face against him.

But what really piqued my curiosity was the fact that the counter-catalyst crystals that normally sealed a rift in space-time weren't actually working. Once I told Zevarius about this, he theorized that it was because all of our rift counter-catalysts were meant to close the ones that Demons made, and the Demons didn't make this one, they just happened to figure out they could use it.

But finding out that the rift was still open seemed to give him an idea or two. He started grabbing materials, and processing aloud just what he was thinking.

"The rift is still open, which means that the pathways themselves remain open, both the ones to Hell, and to home..."

He then looked at the wide-field scan data I had just gathered from scanning the rift.

"...And the Demons are only taking the path from Hell to here. So... if we figure out how to..."

His words were interrupted by the furious scribbling of calculations on a nearby whiteboard.

"...shift the position of the opening itself by... negative X... no... positive X... no... wait... wait..."

I could practically hear his head racing as he pieced together the last parts of the equation. He then grabbed a holographic globe projector from his ship, and hurriedly brought it into the lab, turning it on to reveal a blank sphere.

"All right, the rift is here," Zevarius said, creating a single data point near the center. "The edge of the Dyson

Shield is here, and on the other side of it, this solar system." He continued as he drew a line to represent the barrier. "If the rift were to reposition by two thousand kilometers negative Y, and another five hundred positive Z, which would thankfully put it inside the shield, this would cause its end point to shift back to my reality, and only a hop, skip and a jump from my home world!"

Zevarius seemed quite excited to figure that out. "Only problem is, how do we shove an entire spatial rift like that?" he then questioned.

"What about just creating one of the same type at those coordinates?" I asked. "It'd allow us to safely close the other without worrying about stranding you here."

"Well, that would require a very intense deconstruction of the rift's energies, down to the base sub-thaumetic variance—"

"Like a Deep-Field Scan-Pulse?"

Zevarius sat there for a second as he figured out his universe's equivalent to one of those, then nodded. I of course, informed him that my ship was capable of such a scan, but I'd have to keep it cloaked since I'd need to go outside the Dyson Shield, though it probably wouldn't be a problem since The Unmaker was fighting the Demons coming from the rift, and was unlikely to be looking for hidden vessels, let alone one with as sophisticated a cloaking system as mine.

We met up at the Aura Runner, and after lifting off, set course for the edge of the Dyson Shield nearest to the open rift, while Zevarius kept his servo-sphere on Aldin to continue repairs on the Snap. I cloaked the Aura Runner not long before we were at the barrier, and could see the fight happening outside. Though we figured that The Unmaker's ships were trying to scan the portal as well, we both knew we needed that information of our own, since there was no way those ships were gonna share it with us.

A few of the wrecked ships drifting towards us bounced off of the Aura Runner's shields as we slowly approached, undetected.

"I think you missed a few of them," Zevarius commented.

"I know how to fly my own ship, Zev," I answered. He didn't seem to mind the nickname. But then I realized that we were about to hit a snag. Initial proximity scans showed that once I actually started a deep-field scan, the erratic energy makeup of the rift would cause a reflective resonance that would effectively render the Aura Runner's cloak useless. When I informed Zevarius of this, he was quick to figure out that it means the Demons would start trying to get to the ship. Even as I was pressing the buttons on my console to do so, I explained that I could lower the shields in a specific area of the bigger-on-the-inside cargo bay that would cause Demonic warp-ins to funnel into there, where we could fight them.

"I do hope that arm isn't just for show—" I barely finished saying as the appendage whirred and formed itself into a cannon. "Okay, thank the gods. I would've been really disappointed if you got a whole mechanical arm and it couldn't even double as a cannon."

"Do you think me that boring?" He cheekily replied.

"Not with that shade of blue head-hair. Ready?"

He nodded, and I pressed the button to start the Deep-Field scan-pulse, and lower the shields over where I wanted the Demons to board. Sure enough, the warp-ins were just finishing as we got down.

"Aura guide me, through fire and flood, through friend and foe, that I may emerge in great victory!" I recited my battle prayer I drew my cutlass, and Zev's arm cannon charged.

"This battle, and the death of my foes will bring me *great* honor!" Zevarius called out as a jet-black armor closed itself around his nose and muzzle, and he began firing at the first ones to warp in. I closed the distance on another set, and started cutting them to ribbons.

The first to actually take a swing at me went for a diagonal slash, quickly met with a parry, and a cut across its neck before I skewered up through its head and kicked it down. These were just Bulwark Demons, the infantry of Hell. In chess, the pawns go first, and these were the pawns that went first.

Zevarius soon had to contend with a Whiplance Demon, called so for the protruding prehensile appendages on their back, tipped with a needle-like point. He was surprisingly acrobatic, dodging and flipping around the thing's strikes, and weakening it with shots from his cannon, before a coup-de-grace from the arm as a bayonet shunted from it to aid him with the melee combat.

A few more Bulwarks and now it was my turn to face a tough one. Firesky Demons don't actually fly, but are named such for the fact that they like to shoot fire. A lot. I retaliated with bolts of my own after deflecting the shots with the Borfblade, soon punching enough holes in it to kill, and the fight continued.

An alert from Techbooth. The scan-pulse was twenty percent done. The plan was to jump back into the Dyson Shield as soon as the process was finished, and if The Unmaker's ships hadn't closed the rift by the time we figured out the counter-catalystic frequency, then we'd do it ourselves.

Then trouble came walking through the door. Or rather, warping into the cargo bay. Towering at no less than twenty feet tall was a Monument Breaker, and the flanged mace it wielded was about as tall as myself. Though I dodged the first swing, I rather foolishly tried to brace my sword against my arm to block the follow-up, and ended up catapulted into the wall from the sheer force as Zevarius looked over at it and cursed.

The bugger was still focused on me, though, and I was ducking and rolling around its legs and slashing at those until one of them swung up and punted me back into the wall like a can getting kicked across the road. With my right hand conjuring a shield, I held back the subsequent pounding that it tried to give me with that mace as I waited for my ribs to put themselves back together with haste.

With the shattering of a glass bottle, the Monument Breaker roared in pain as it turned around towards Zevarius, and I saw just what it was he did. Whatever was in the flask he threw, it was melting straight through the Demon's skin, muscle, and bone. With it now distracted, I quickly righted myself and sliced at the air with the Borfblade, channeling The Aura through it to cleave through the enemy's leg, causing it to leave its own foot behind as it tried to step forward, and collapse on the ground. Zevarius then charged his cannon for a more powerful shot, and there wasn't much left of the thing's head once he let it loose.

"Go back to the shadow, waste," Zevarius spat.

The scan-pulse was only fifty percent done by this point, and Demons were still trying to warp in. You'd think they'd figure out that one ship isn't worth the amount of guys they were losing. Then again, it is the Aura Runner, and the Demons likely encountered it more than a few times during the First War for Reality, and its previous pilots. But then wouldn't that make it the case that they'd figure out that they really can't take the Aura Runner?

A few more tougher-than-average Bulwarks were my next opponent. These guys had found their favored weapons beyond the apparently standard-issue warhammer or arming sword, and I really do hate facing opponents with smallswords, so I bolted the Bulwark wielding one until he was no longer standing as I continued to employ retreating parries against the other two, soon finding opportunities to strike their weapon hands with quick, snapping blows. In Eskrima, we call those *watiks*, based on the onomatopoeia. Smack their weapon hand, and the weapon will generally fall out from it. Especially since I did it with a cutlass, and there was now a fair amount of those hands no longer attached.

Zevarius dealt with his next group by switching firing

modes of his arm cannon, and the beam made quick work of the battle line that was advancing against him. I heard him also comment "Were it not for the fact we are indoors, I would be using the missiles!"

"I appreciate you not obliterating my cargo bay!" I replied.

By the time the scan-pulse was done, Zevarius and I were about ankle-deep in Demon's blood, with plenty spattered on our clothes and armors. Nothing a good shower couldn't fix, though, and I do have one onboard.

But anyways, we got what we needed, and not long after the Aura Runner phase-jumped back into the safety of the Dyson Shield, The Unmaker's forces closed the rift themselves. Thank the gods we got the scan done when we did.

All that was left was to actually process and interpret the data, which was a calm walk in the park compared to the haste that was getting ahold of it.

As I postulated how to make the portal of those specific energies, I paced about the lab. I had no desire to make any more Rune Bricks than I needed for the Way Gate to the Field of Unreality, to which Zevarius was quite understanding. There were undoubtedly other ways to make a portal of that kind, stable enough for him and the *Snap* to get through, I just needed to figure out what it was.

But speaking of Rune Bricks, Zevarius approached me with what looked like one of our Veldenite Chisels, but modified. After his explanation, I realized just what he had done for us. He'd managed to create a supersaturated form of the Veldenite compound, that upon contact with one of the bricks, would stabilize back into its solid state, thus imprinting itself onto the brick, without having to manually chisel each symbol. The idea of Veldenite stamps on Rune Bricks had actually become viable. All you had to do was dip and press. Not only had he managed this, he even created such stamps for all twenty-seven of the base glyphs used in Rune Brick energy manipulation. Dude had turned a ten to twelve-year job into a two-week one, and had made detailed instructions on how to make the metastable Veldenite compound to boot.

"Honestly, this could reinvigorate Rune Bricks as a form of Psionic architecture," I told him. "It's been falling out of favor simply for its sheer tediousness, and you just made yourself the fucking Johannes Gutenberg of the craft," I informed him. "I owe you big for this. Hell, the whole universe does."

"Figure out that portal and I will consider all debts paid," Zevarius said with a cathartic chuckle. "I am only an alchemist, it is you who are the Psionic."

"See, this is why cross-discipline cooperation is so damned important," I commented as I looked at the readout on the rift's energetic makeup. "If I were to modify one of my Pulsar Missiles to carry a payload of this energetic resonance, it would punch a hole in space-time that would essentially have the rift back to your reality as its crater."

Zevarius seemed only slightly skeptical of the idea, because he wasn't sure how one would confirm that it was even the correct rift type. But as soon as I said that it would likely even be possible to see to the other side from how long the rift would be stable for, he had a lot more faith in it. It indeed would be pretty neat to be able to get visual confirmation that we did things right, rather than having to take a leap of faith. I don't like leaps of faith. They're annoying. Zevarius seemed to share this sentiment.

Just as quickly as I mentioned how long it might take just to program the modifications, Zevarius's servo-sphere piped up, and the ball of helpfulness had a point. As a pure machine computer, it could much more quickly execute the operations than I could, and turn a two-day programming job into a few minutes at most.

I gave the servo-sphere access to the missile I intended to use, and he got right on the job, and the beeps almost sounded like his version of humming as he worked.

"I cannot thank you enough for what you are about to achieve for me," Zevarius brought up to me as the sphere worked.

"Don't thank me yet, we haven't yet figured out for sure if it works," I reminded.

"If it does work, there will not be enough time for expressions of gratitude and goodbyes before I have to make the trip," Zevarius then pointed out. He was right. Once we saw that his home planet was on the other side of the rift, he'd have a minute at most before the stability of the rift would make the trip anything other than perfectly safe.

The servo-sphere beeped a few times to tell us the job was finished. I gave him a few more pats for the job well done, which he definitely appreciated before hovering back into the Dropship *Snap*.

"Perhaps we will meet again someday, when you have defeated The Unmaker, and our universes' technologies will allow more... intentional visits," Zevarius started. "It may be a while though, and I only know that *I* will live that long."

"Do I really look like the kind of person who dies?" I asked him, to a solid and genuine laugh. "But seriously, I'll live to see the day with The Aura as my power."

"Then Aura guide you, Radien."

"And honor to you, Zevarius. I won't downplay it, you may have very well just ensured our victory against The Unmaker."

With an exchange of salutes, myself offering the Death Worlder's, and him with his clan's, everything was ready. Our ships met up at the coordinates to open the rift. I fired off the modified Pulsar Missile, and sure enough, the portal not only opened, but I could even see the other side, which Zevarius confirmed was exactly where he needed to get to. Another quick farewell, and the *Snap* flew through the portal, which destabilized and shut about ninety seconds later.

What a lad. What a fucking legendary dude, singlehandedly knocking off a good ten years from the timetable, and possibly being the catalyst of a resurgence in Rune Brick Psionic Architecture.

I later went out to the site we were planning to build the Way Gate on, a grassy knoll just outside a cool-looking forest. But something felt off about those woods, and I couldn't really explain it, even to myself. My instincts boosted by The Aura tipped me off that something wasn't right over there. And since Zevarius's aid took that much off of our workload, I definitely had the time to investigate. Besides, I couldn't help but feel a strong urge to make sure that there wasn't anything that could possibly interfere with the Way Gate's construction.

Sure, the forest was over there, and the Way Gate would be in the field, but I had the time to not take the chance, and assure that there was harmony in the land both at the gate, and surrounding it.

With The Aura's Sight, I saw that there was a Font in the forest. One of those places where raw cosmic power coalesces, and I began to make my way towards it. But the hairs on the back of my neck were standing on end, and I knew I wasn't the only intelligence in these woods.

I stopped in my tracks, hand on the hilt of my cutlass. And at the moment it counted, I unsheathed it, spinning around to point it right at the spirit I could sense nearby. The shadowy visage also stopped in its tracks, with no interest in throwing itself on my sword.

"I have no desire to destroy you," I said aloud to it, hoping it could understand me. Just in case it couldn't, I decided to be the first person to take my hand off the trigger, and sheathed the Borfblade.

The spirit walked around me, stopping to place itself between us and the Font. Now that I knew that something was up here, I left the forest to consult anyone who had a clue.

Jarrek was the one to point me to an archaeologist specializing in Psionic Phenomena, a Hajikahl named Pyrhea, whom last he heard, had resumed work at a site on Laksor. With the Dyson Shield making sure that The Unmaker wasn't getting in anytime soon, day-to-day life in the Velani Array for those not specifically working towards the effort against The Unmaker had more or less resumed.

I contacted Pyrhea, my initial message containing a dossier on what I had observed of the spirit, and my inquiry hoping that she could help me out. The next day, I got a reply, and we began our discussion as soon as the visual link was established. I admittedly couldn't help but blurt out "Oh whoa, big fluffy fire doggo" when I first saw her, because that's honestly a pretty apt descriptor of a Hajikahl. Though three of the four species of the Haji-Son family were feline, the Hajikahl were the exception. But they were still considered Haji-Son since they're from the Nashira Strand, like the Hajivakk, Hajinehr and Hajitorr, and the lot of them are all pretty tight-knit in their relations.

Pyrhea chuckled as she asked if I had never seen a Hajikahl before, to which I replied "I've met Hajikahl before, you're just very tall," to which she thanked me as I realized that comments about height were considered compliments to the Hajikahl. That goes for both tallness and shortness, by the way. It's like saying 'You carry yourself well.'

But on to business, Pyrhea informed me that I was most likely dealing with a Spirit of Scorn in those woods. The Font that existed there was likely corrupted, which I hadn't noticed in my initial look with The Aura's Sight. Pyrhea pointed out that it most likely meant that the Font had been corrupted for so long, it looks like the normal state of it now.

She forwarded me detailed information about Spirits of Scorn, along with how to release them to the beyond. According to the notes, it was most likely that the spirit was the actual person who corrupted the Font in life, and now protects the rest of the universe from it out of shame.

So now with this new knowledge, I headed back into the forest, straight towards the Font, that with a second look, I could see that it had been corrupted. As soon as I approached the cave, I found myself hurtled back by the outstretched arm of the Spirit of Scorn. I stood back up, and looked at its ghostly form.

"I know what you are, and that you can understand me," I said to it, brushing myself off. "And I swear on my charge and honor as an Aura Warrior, I will cleanse this Font, and bring you peace."

It stood there for a moment, before stepping aside and letting me pass. I had never seen a corrupted Font before, and I can tell you, I definitely could've gone my whole life without doing so and felt no worse for it.

The whole place was just... existing wrong. An eerie red glow lit the cavern as its walls seemed to slowly bleed red and black bile, and the font itself, which normally looked like a natural well of cosmic energy, pulsed with... wretchedness. I could hear the sounds of its pain, a heartbeat too loud to be anything but disturbing, and a quietly wailing chorus like it was straight from a brimstone pit full of the damned.

"What the hell did you do?" I asked the spirit as I turned around to face it again. It placed its shadowy hand on my shoulder, and I was flung back into a memory from long ago.

The arcanist at the Font was of the genetic precursor to the Laksorian species, the Lagastir. And he was pissed, if the Psionic Ritual he was performing wasn't a hint enough.

*"To you I pour my hate, my rage..."* He chanted, his voice seething with the kind of anger that comes when no one believes you when you're telling the truth. *"Bring forth fire and death to they who mocked me, who disparaged me, who called all but their disciplines worthless and out of time..."*

Some of Aldin Moon's history included the vicious divide between those who studied Psionic Sciences, and those who studied Technological Sciences; that became the Academy Wars of the Sixth Cosmic Era. Both fields had seen massive leaps and bounds in development and discovery as they tried to push ahead of the other in polarizing competition, eventually boiling over and leading to what is now regarded as one of the civilized universe's darkest chapters.

This was one of the single most massive losses of life in the entire conflict. The whole continent became awash in the fire and death this Arcanist summoned in corrupting the Font. So much so, that a group of Arch-Magi, who used to be on his side, were the ones to put an end to him. They bound him to the Font with their own hate and rage, that he mocked them and disparaged them with how he went too far. He went too far just to be able to say his discipline wasn't worthless and out of time.

When I snapped out of the vision, my breath was slow and steady as I processed it all.

"I swore I would bring you peace," I said to the Spirit of Scorn, not even looking over. "As much as I now question the wisdom in that, a promise is a promise, and a billion and a third years is a long time to think about what you've done."

I looked over to the Font, latching on to the Corrupted Heart of the Flood with The Aura. "It will be up to the gods to decide whether or not that's long enough."

I began to pull at the corrupted heart like an old nail from a board, tugging at the root of evil that poisoned this flow of the universe's lifeblood, and soon saw a crimson orb shoot from the Font itself, and form into a specter as it hit the ground and took shape.

"And who are you?" I said aloud just before it conjured a weapon. I could only finish that with "Oh, okay then," switching the tether to my right hand as I drew my sword with my dominant one to defend myself, and tear this corruption out by its roots.

The shade that attacked me was quickly met with a parry and two diagonal slashes across its body, followed by a kick to push it away, and almost immediately afterwards, I was beset by two more.

Moving around the cavern while holding onto the tether was not easy, but it was doable, and I ended up retreating into a corner so the two attackers couldn't get to my flanks. A cornered rattlesnake is the most dangerous kind, and the new assailants were dispatched soon enough.

But as soon as three new specters flung themselves from the Font, I was getting fed up with the multitasking, and yanked as hard as I could to rip the Corrupted Heart of the

Flood out from the Font, and just as one of the leaping ghostly foes would've met their mark, I succeeded, and dispelled the foes that were throwing themselves at me.

In solving one problem, though, I was holding on to another. The pulsing orb of hate was unstable as hell, and it was taking a lot of strain on me just to hold it together. I ran out from the cavern and used my Comm-Link to call Pyrhea, who thankfully answered.

"Good of you to answer, Pyrhea," I said with as calm a demeanor I could muster through the exertion. "Time-sensitive question, how to destroy a Corrupted Heart of the Flood?"

I saw Pyrhea's eyes widen with urgency as I asked, and she sprang up from her chair, charging towards a terminal back at the university of Kleidar on Laksor, ordering her colleagues out of the way and even knocking one over on accident. In her defense though, it generally is not a good idea to be in the path of a sprinting seven-foot-tall pyrokinetic canine with a very impressive mane and neck fluff.

She quickly briefed me on what to do, and thankfully it was pretty simple. After running back into the field outside the forest, I heaved the orb as hard as I could into the air, and dropped back my stance to conjure a full blast, like the one I used against the Opponent Unbeatable almost five hundred years ago now.

The Corrupted Heart of the Flood was headed right for me on its way down, since I was the closest thing it could try to latch on to and take possession. But I fired the sphere I had charged right at it, causing a spectacular explosion of red, blue and purple as the powers battled each other and soon dispersed.

I turned around, heading back to the edge of the forest, where the Spirit of Scorn had been watching from.

"It's done. You can go now," I told it, and it faded away as it bowed its translucent head.

I headed back to the Font, and saw the cavern as it should be, achieved for the first time in a painfully long time. The azure glow of the cracks and seams of the stone walls had returned, and the cistern of raw universe flowed freely again.

Upon returning to the field, I saw two of the Laksorians who were helping make the Rune Bricks looking very concerned.

"Don't worry, that was the fix," I told them, to which Kela and Damon nodded in a 'fair enough' sort of manner.

Work continued, and I even found myself reciting a ridiculous old tune from when I'd make bagels from scratch at the Fourteen Werewolves...

*It's the Bagels of Destruction!*
*Free at last from New York dungeon!*
*It's the Bagels of Destruction!*
*Their bloodlust will fill the oceans!*
*They came from the depths of a place I preferred*
*when it was called New Amsterdam,*
*Their directive, like their homeland's,*
*to bring forth misery and death!*
*A paradox to be sure, but*
*among the few things they did right,*
*Was the reversal of the polarity of*

*this mission of the darkest night!*
*It's the Bagels of Destruction!*
*Free at last from New York dungeon!*
*It's the Bagels of Destruction!*
*Their bloodlust will fill the oceans!*
*Like Prometheus before me*
*I give the gift of knowledge to Man,*
*Thus I bring to fall the grip that*
*unworthy hands once had!*
*Though their secret is no longer, they can take solace,*
*That their ideals aren't the worst of the lot,*
*just look at Georgia, Florida, or Texas!*
*It's the Bagels of Destruction!*
*They know neither mercy nor reduction!*
*It's the Bagels of Destruction!*
*No longer secret their construction!*

Anyways, I only got about halfway through the second chorus before I realized that the entire Laksorian team was watching with great amusement, in no small part because we had actually finished the bricks, and they were taking bets on how many extra ones I'd make before realizing we were finished. Zevarius's Veldenite stamps had really sped up the process. We were looking at more like five entire ASC (a little over fifteen Earth years) more to get them all done otherwise.

"I uh... I guess we've got them all, then," I said with a bit of red in my cheeks.

I had made five extra bricks in my stupor, in case you were wondering. Also, yes, they were called, "The Bagels of Destruction" on the menu of the Fourteen Werewolves. It had its place among other well-named items, such as the Toast Skagen I called, "The Toast of Glorious Death," and the "Borfburger," which was a pretty potent burger indeed.

Look, it's not like I actually had to worry about making a profit, okay? I was having fun with it. But that aside, we finished the damn bricks. Also, don't ask me how I was getting good shrimp out in the Midwest.

...Okay, fine, I was teleporting to and from the coast. It beat the alternative.

But with the bricks for both the circle and the arches finished, as well as the mundane runes around the ring to bind it all together ready, I called a meeting of the lot of us.

Myself, Veralis, Jarrek, Micah, Miirkae, Dorg, Arakai, Jaden, Xenidar. The nine heads of the universe's remaining resistance were together in one room to make ready the final push. Technically, only six of us were in the room. Xenidar was just a hologram partaking remotely from Turazin, but he was present all the same. That also went for Miirkae and Dorg, they were still running the Fortress Borfus on Raon-Arashal.

Much as we could've just used the Warp Obelisks that existed between our planets to achieve us all in the same room, it would've been kinda silly since we could just have the meeting like this.

"All of the Rune Bricks for the Way Gate to the Field of Unreality are prepared," I started. "I haven't begun the construction yet, because as soon as I do, it won't be long before The Unmaker realizes what's going on, and brings the might of the universe to bear against us."

"Okay, but how exactly is he gonna know?" Miirkae

asked. "He doesn't have operatives inside the Velani Dyson Shield, or it would've already fallen."

"The placing of the Rune Bricks will mean that they begin emitting their specific energies immediately," Jaden explained. "I'd estimate Radien will be able to place about a quarter of the base circle, including the binding ring before The Unmaker puts two and two together from the micro-fluctuations that will start happening within his domain."

"Basically right now, what we're doing is tearing a hole into the wall instead of trying to find the door," I further elaborated. "He's gonna start hearing us tapping with the hammer before we start to swing it."

"All of his forces will undoubtedly converge on the Dyson Shield, but there's right now no way to know where they'll show up," Dorg pointed out. "I suggest you create an artificial weak point in the grid itself to ensure where the convergence will be. Granted, The Unmaker would undoubtedly notice the trap if the shield was simply lowered. There would have to be an actual malfunction, just not naturally created."

"Dorg's right," I affirmed. "The Unmaker is as opportunistic as he is clever. He'd take advantage of a buckle in the shield, but would absolutely see a baited line."

"I can make sure we give him the opportunity he wants," Jarrek said. "There are ways that the Dyson Shield could naturally have minor malfunctions like the ones he'd take advantage of. We'll have our bait, don't worry."

"All right then," I concurred. "My plan is to lay the base circle by hand, as well as the first few feet of the arches.

Once my hands alone can no longer get that high, I'll start having to lift the bricks telekinetically. Of course, Rune Bricks are not easy to lift with telekinesis, it's part of their design. I'll be able to do two at a time safely, at most. But the bulk of the construction is the circle, so it's actually gonna take less time since the bricks will naturally bind together once their ends meet. No mortar required, thank the gods."

"What about a combined effort with the construction we've all got?" Xenidar suggested. "You sent both The Hideout and the Fortress the schematics, and I know that my team's almost finished making their own bricks with the Veldenite stamps your interdimensional friend invented. Besides, The Hideout's better defended than an entire solar system. No offense, Arch-Militant."

"None taken, you're correct." Jarrek chuckled.

"That would be a lot more viable if The Unmaker didn't have almost literally *all* the armies," Micah cut in. "He's got the manpower to send more than enough ships to each planet to flatten them all. The Way Gates you guys are almost ready are for in case we fail over here on Aldin."

"As far as he'll know, there's only gonna be one bunch looking to get into his turf. And it's honestly in our interest to keep it that way for now," I added. "Unfortunately, you guys at The Hideout and Torvaltyne Bastion need every hand on deck yourselves, so reinforcements via the Warp Obelisks are out of the question once things get started."

"But we could use help in setting the traps," Jarrek said. "We've got until that first brick goes down to get the defense ready, laying down cloaked EMP mines, Vortex

Emulators, Subspace Vacuole Generators... the name of the game is stalling The Unmaker's armies, buying as much time as possible for the Way Gate to finish construction."

"Radien, my team will help you with the circle, and evacuate once you start working on the arches, since they're not power-wielders themselves," Jaden noted, and I nodded. That would be helpful. With the bulk of the structure being the circle, getting that done as quickly as possible would be instrumental.

"Admirable as your reluctance to use lethal force is, Jarrek, The Unmaker is not likely to share that restraint," Miirkae pointed out. "True as it is that he has made no properly military action against anyone, that will likely change with a direct threat making itself known."

"Acknowledged, Miirkae," Jarrek responded. "I've told my pilots to avoid it if they can help it, but if push comes to shove, it's us or him." He then sighed. "As much as we're gonna be fighting our own friends, everyone in every ship that'll be there, our side or The Unmaker's, at one point or another, accepted *themselves* what risks come with stepping into those cockpits for *any* reason."

"If the Velani defense starts to buckle, evacuations will take place until the instant one of those ships makes planetfall," Micah continued. "After that, you three will need to destroy the Warp Obelisks you've got connected to Redaria Prime, then you're on your own."

Xenidar, Miirkae and Dorg all nodded. The table fell silent as we all mentally prepared for the final push against The Unmaker, then I piped up.

"I will be gathering power until we're ready to begin," I said, to no one's protest. "I'll probably be the first of the strike team to get into the gate, and I gotta be ready for anything. Aura guide us all."

With that, the meeting adjourned, and we all went to our stations. With the Font in the forest restored and cleansed, that was where I was going to meditate until the time to take on The Unmaker had come.

Inside the small natural cavern, I saw the universe's lifeblood seeping through... well, I really can't say a wound in space, because then that would sound bad. It was more like a natural runoff reservoir that was concentrated enough to physically manifest. The raw power of The Aura, Psionics itself... I don't think I'll ever get used to the sight, let alone tired of it.

I knelt down, sitting myself into a meditative position, and called the raw power of the cosmos to flow through me.

I thought about talking to you at this point, Effigy. But I had kinda set myself on telling you the story once it was over. I mean, I sort of am, darkly humorous as that is. With no offense to you, I contacted the Aura Prism instead. Cynofrax's people may have fallen to The Unmaker, but the Prism was far more resilient. We spoke in a canvas realm, where we could be face-to-face remotely, and without the possible intrusion of The Unmaker.

Face... to face. Heh, that actually still works for this one.

The Prism was actually quite perturbed by the fact that The Unmaker's plan was working, and was exceptionally relieved to hear my uncorrupted voice.

"Do you have *any* idea how infuriating it is to be surrounded by a population consisting exclusively of the radical zealots of a corrupter that wants nothing but the enslavement of all they see?" was the Prism's opening statement.

I heartily responded *"Yes!"* as the Prism remembered that I was from Earth once. But I briefed him on what was about to happen.

...

Okay, I *know* that the prism can't be a him or her, but when I'm hearing the Prism's voice, it's a male voice. Maybe it's different for other people. Gimme a break. The Prism has never minded the pronoun.

But anyways, I gave the Prism the lowdown on our efforts, and was glad that he hadn't been himself corrupted by The Unmaker. The Prism was quick to remind me that his role was to maintain the barriers between the universe and the Burning Hells, and letting the Demons in freely was not conducive to The Unmaker's plan.

"I wish there was a way I could help from here, but with my efforts focused entirely on keeping The Mountain safe, and the refugees within its caverns, I cannot risk faltering my own energies. I'm... not even sure how I would even help you once it began."

I chuckled and told the Prism I didn't expect outright assistance, and he *immediately* called me out, sternly saying, "You're planning to face him alone."

I didn't know what else to say. "I don't know what to

expect once I enter the Field of Unreality. For all I know, it's gonna be an endless army of death that awaits me, and I'd really rather not subject my allies to getting as overwhelmed as I would suddenly be. Besides, one person can sneak through an area. A squad of seven's a bit harder to conceal once inside."

"I get it," The Prism told me, but in a tone that definitely suggested he didn't agree with my plan. "There are advantages and disadvantages to either side of that equation. If I were under the impression that you would scout the area, return, then tell the rest of your team to accompany you, that'd be a much more tactical plan. But I also know you well enough Radien, to know that if you think you've got the chance to do it yourself, without even risking your allies having to be put in such an unknown form of danger, you'll do it."

"Is that bad?" I asked the Prism. "If I'm the only thing that's risked, I think that's way better than risking myself, *and* all of them."

"I have no answer for that, because there is no solid yes or no to it," The Prism replied. "Like I said, both have their advantages and disadvantages. I'm not going to try to convince you otherwise of something you've already made up your mind on. The best I can do is hope that whatever decision you've made, it turns out to be the one that works. And if it does, that will only be further cause for celebration, that your skill paid off."

I sighed with relief. "I can't think of any better thing you could say to me. Thank you. For trusting me to know what

I'm doing."

"I do not doubt your skill, Radien. Not for one moment. Nor do I doubt your cleverness, your determination, your honor or your ideals," The Prism started. "I also understand just what your enemies are willing to do in the pursuit of defeating you."

I nodded. It really is annoying to be the only person in the group who doesn't mind himself dying. The Prism and I continued to talk for a bit as I continued my meditation in the Font, and I figured most of the energy I was absorbing would go into lifting the Rune Bricks into place, and my 'normal' amount would be left over to deal with The Unmaker, to which the Prism concurred, and commended the tactical idea.

I like tactics. Tactics are good.

One of the Laksorian assistants was actually the one to poke me out of my meditation. Torden informed me that it had been nine days since I entered the cave, and everything was set and ready, and the time was now. I nodded, walking back with him to the meadow we were going to construct the Way Gate in. Once I got there, I rolled my shoulders, and looked at the tables with the bricks, the map of the layout, and the journals they were discerned from. The rest of the team Jaden was lending me were still on their way, and I had a bit of time, so I flipped through one of the diaries of Alia Mev-Rossar, and noticed something odd. There was a small watermark on one of the corners of one of the empty last pages, and I looked at it again with The Aura's Sight, so I could discern just what was going on.

Turned out, there was a hidden entry to the diary

here, and on the remaining pages. Alia had used something similar to one of my Autotelekinetic Cantrips to pen an entry that could only be seen by... well, someone like me, who can do this sort of thing, and who would bother to figure it out. The Aura translated the entry for me, written in the modern (at the time) Cevian script, instead of the coded Althrak like everything else was.

*I grow tired of codes, weary of ciphers. That I must disguise these words of mine... it weighs heavily on my soul. And as a Cevian of science, it is not easy for any matter to do such. Arigen Concarius left me with very specific instructions for how to proceed after he stepped through that gateway, including what to do if he should fail to return. But he did return, telling me he found something far more profound than his 'save-state universe.' He called it the Canvas Realm, and after brief revelry, became solemn. We both knew that this place, and control over it and access to it could be the seeds of a conflict to rival the bloodshed of the Sentience War. A place of infinite malleability, where the only limit to what existed was your will, your imagination. The universe could set itself ablaze fighting over the right to own it.*

*So he ordered me to hide the schematics for the gateway, by any means I saw fit. And after he returned to that realm, the gateway was to be destroyed. He even told me exactly how to do so in a way that would seem as though he mysteriously disappeared while testing his theories. I wouldn't even be in the building when it happened if I did my part right. Exactly two days after I did what he asked, his vanishing took place, in circumstances as puzzling to all others as he anticipated.*

*I am not burdened by my being accessory to this, nor I am burdened by what followed, even as whole galaxies seemed so enthralled by the mysterious disappearance of Arigen Concarius. What happened to Arigen Concarius? The question of a generation was set, and being his most trusted assistant, I knew that I would not be spared from fame. Though I never actively wished for it, I didn't reject it outright. I knew how to make sure I never divulged the secret of Arigen's 'disappearance,' let alone even hint at the very existence of a secret. But as time went on, a different nagging problem began to creep into my mind, and become what burdens me now.*

*For it, I find myself in this cave, on a world hardly anyone remembers the name of, having fled a city that came under the crossfire of three different invading stellar pirate factions. Having so carefully chosen every word I spoke aloud, with just as much care with every step I took that others could see, all in the name of finally managing to vanish, just like Arigen did. Admittedly it was a lot easier for him to pull it off.*

*I slowly smuggled these journals with me over these last years until this cave finally contained my life's work, with nobody knowing where it, or I am. I have once again attained the obscurity I had while working with Arigen.*

*But in my twilight years, my mind grows tired, so I will no longer shadow my thoughts and regrets with a tide of words. That is what has burdened me now. I know it sounds crazy, I still find it hard to convince myself that it isn't... but I'm tired of complexity. Well, not that exactly... I'm tired of being clever. I've been clever all my life, from when I first showed promise as a pupil of science, to when I was accepted into the academy I studied at, to my career in a respected field of Psionic sciences. I've not once in all my life ever had the chance to just... but in this cavern, I am finally safe to just turn my damn brain off.*

The rest of that final page consisted entirely of sentences no more than ten words long, simply worded and without any bother to elaborate, that basically spilled Alia's very soul onto the paper. A lot of 'I wish I was,' followed typically by a trait or even an emotional state. There were a few 'I would have liked to,' or 'I like to' statements as well, all of them very simply written, like the words were taken from the vocabulary of a child. And yet, it was the kind of simplicity that somehow resonated, likely because Alia Mev-Rossar had been so eloquent in all of his writings until then. The sudden drop of all subtlety and facade, as if he was now treating using bigger words as a form of secrecy itself... it was as odd as it was harrowing, the fact that I had found myself thinking about it so hard, both then and now.

Fortunately, it had killed just the right amount of time for the group Jaden sent to arrive, and it was now time to get to business.

"You all know what you're doing, and how to do it?" I asked. They nodded. "Once the first ring is finished, I'll start working on the arches as the rest of you finish the circle. Let's go!"

Immediately, we began placing down the bricks of the first inner ring. The mundane runes that bound the construction together as an actual proper circle had been placed already, since they could be done without anyone noticing, let alone The Unmaker. We moved quickly, and within the first minute, the first outer ring was placed. I started immediately placing the first bricks of the arches, running from position to position to stick them end-to-end in the planned order. It was pure synergy, and it was satisfying as hell, despite the circumstances.

All of us were running past each other in perfect order, not a single collision as we hastily put the bricks down. Soon, I had to start the heavy lifting with my mind, literally. The arches had grown too tall for me to just plain reach, and there was no way in hell I was gonna climb it. Not that I couldn't, it just really would not have made any difference. So two at a time, I'd grab bricks and lift them up into position onto the arches. And it was a damn good thing I had meditated for the past nine days straight in front of a Font, or I would've been exhausted by the time the first dozen had been planted. But thanks to that preplanning of mine, I just kept going, and so did the Laksorians.

As anticipated, they finished the circle before I finished the arches, and so I thanked them that their work was done, and advised them to get going, which they did. With only half of the arches finished, though, I got a message from Veralis over the comm-link.

"The first ships have arrived at the edge of the Dyson Shield," she informed. "They're starting to gather. Exemplar Kendro-Dalinor is leading them."

As soon as I heard that name, I realized aloud "Ooh, He's not going to be happy about that once this is over..."

Acknowledging Veralis's communication and advising

everyone to stall for time, I continued. The last lift I needed to do was the single connecting apex piece for the four arches, which looked like a big stone runic plus sign. And it sure had heft to match, both in my hands and off the ground.

But as soon as it made contact with its resting place, The whole assembly glowed with a harmonic toll, and I placed my hand on the gemstone between the four bricks in the center to activate the whole thing with a pulse of what I could best describe as 'blank energy.'

I stepped back as the pulse traveled through the bricks along the rings, circling the innermost, then to the next, then continuing outward as the base energy was altered with each symbol it passed through, bumped this way and that, tuned with utmost precision.

When the pulse reached the first arch, it rocketed up the length, then back down another side, back up once more, and then finally back down to rocket across the mundane runes along the edge to the next arch in the same manner, and then the third, and finally the fourth, running up, then down, then up again, but speeding across the final two faces at the same time in a zigzag, to converge at the apex and be flung downwards onto the center one last time, tearing a hole in space itself as it opened the portal like a zipper through the fabric of the universe itself.

The glowing portal awaited, fringes of white energy crackling around its edge, and a deep blue vortex in the center, leading to the Field of Unreality.

"Thank the gods it worked," I said with a very relieved sigh. I took the comm-link out of my pocket, ready to tell

Veralis and the others that the Way Gate was active. But I then found myself staring into the portal, remembering my whole conversation with the Aura Prism as I simultaneously remembered that my plan was to go alone. I weighed the options one last time. I had the whole damn debate again for the ten seconds that it took to run through all the points, consider them all, and then make my decision as I set the comm-link on one of the tables, and stepped inside, the Borfblade on my hip, and my Talisman around my neck.

# PART 3
## ENTER DEFENDER

Now inside the Field of Unreality, what I beheld could only mean that The Unmaker had been here for a very long time. A sprawling cityscape, filled with... what I could best describe as "almost people." They existed, and acted exactly as living creatures of their species would, but they weren't actually alive or present. Like a holographic companion that a ship has for its lone pilot to interact with. And it perfectly simulated a city, that had developed, and had a history. My Talisman still protecting me from his lure, now in the heart of the flood, I pressed forth.

But the denizens of Unreality were vigilant, and they had noticed me. I could tell I wasn't unwelcome, just... unexpected. A living soul in a world of simulated ones, that seemed to have been tailor-made to act as the living part of an unliving world... Remember what I said about a holographic companion for the lone pilot to interact with? It was like that, a whole city for its sole occupant to live within, and I had no doubt that The Unmaker regularly interacted with this city, one might suspect he was out and about at that very moment if it weren't for the fact that I traced the only other living energy marker to a massive pyramid at the center of it all. This was The Unmaker's bastion, and the seat of his power.

One of the denizens came up to me and asked me if I was from the outside, like The Unmaker. But they addressed him as Creator. Not The Creator, just Creator. I told them that indeed, I was from that reality beyond this one, and he looked around for a few moments before asking me if I was here to cure him of his sickness.

I inquired further, wondering what he meant. He said that people didn't talk about it amongst themselves, but since I was not from here, I could be told without disgrace that 'for the longest time, Creator would walk with us, and the boundaries of our lands were endless.' But apparently after leaving Unreality for a time, he came back with an air of dread about him, and locked himself into his pyramid. After the equivalent of a little over two million years of his isolation, the cities and the societies that The Unmaker had built began to fade, and now only this last city remained, and even that was decaying as more and more of his power went into his incursion on my universe rather than sustaining his.

So I told him that I would end his sickness, but I also told him of the dilemma that now suddenly faced me, clearly these people had become sentient over The Unmaker's time here, and to destroy The Unmaker would be to destroy them all. But he seemed to know even before I told him, and assured me that what needed to be done, needed to be done. For until The Unmaker banished himself into the pyramid, nobody ever had to wonder how they existed, and why. But after two million years, people now had the time to question and wonder. And question they did, and they had found their answers, in all their solipsistic horror.

So I pressed forth. I moved towards the pyramid, and soon headed inside. I was ready to fight an army of guards, but almost disturbingly, there were none. Ascending flights of stairs in the maze of the pyramid, The Aura guided me towards my goal, illuminating a path that would lead to The Unmaker.

I entered the chamber I knew in my heart of hearts, my mind of minds, would be the throne of The Unmaker. And there he sat, immobile and unconscious in an apparatus that allowed him to Psionically project his will into the universe, and this plan of his, that I still had yet to understand why it existed. The Unmaker was a Draconian—of a kind I'd never seen before, and ancient. Primal and powerful, as was the damage he was doing to history.

Projections of the history of time and its heroes were across the walls. But instead of the bravest souls who earned those victories and made those last stands, it was him in all of them. The nine Universal Defenders were simply becoming one—The Unmaker. Their victories, he was stealing. Kirinaultr's sacrifice at Sehlsaln Anchor, Xatrial Isenhart's creation of the Manifest of Apocalypse, Ahron Kasven—The first of them all, and how he discovered that Hunderfold blades could permanently kill Demons... they were all being turned to just this one Draconian, The Unmaker.

I could see events I had read about, events that were well catalogued being rewritten in front of my eyes, the second Defender, Shpargen-Shperg, and how she wrote the very foundations of wielding Cosmic Power, almost quite literally—she wrote The Keys to Power, a series of manuals that detailed the use of powers that would later be known as The Aura, The Chainbreaker, The *Thuul,* and so many other names. The Unmaker was writing himself in these images, where once there was an honored Hydenti warrior and Defender.

Farrox Tesamaug, the fourth Defender... He saved the universe multiple times from artifacts far too dangerous to be in anyone's possession, hidden them away in an impossible vault that has only even been theorized. Now The Unmaker was taking the Void Cortex, the Dimension Cutter, the Haywire Shield, and locking them away forever, to the relieved applause of the galaxies.

The sixth Defender, Peldane Thari, a Kendrosian—He saw so much history, and helped write so much of it, and now his visage was replaced with The Unmaker. His Kendrosian successor, Thayvek Rentarili, who wrote The Pillars Three! Thayvek penned the words that make the standard that recognizes new sentient life! And now The Unmaker was the one who was scribing those words, to the throngs on Killentarn, and from Varenthiil to Raon-Arashal, to Kalisaine and... and everywhere in between and beyond! A moment no respectable historian would forget, and now everyone was remembering it wrong!

T'Sen Torgaen, the eighth of the line, who lived longer than any other, and is widely regarded as the greatest warrior of them all, now The Unmaker was assuming his titles, and his claims to skill... Even Caltoran, who died valiantly at the hands of Demons, but then corrupted... that was no longer what happened. Caltoran never lived, there was only The Unmaker...

I could hear his voice in my mind now, daring me to forget the names, challenging me to wonder what it'd be like to imagine him as the hero of all the stories instead. How dare he say that I should call him the hero!

"To hell with your madness!" I shouted to the seemingly sedate Dragon on the monolithic throne. "You dare insult me by thinking that I, of all people will forget the names of my allies?! You seriously think yourself beyond those who've done well by me?! You really believe yourself able to upheave *everyone I remember who gave me the time of the fucking day?!*"

I could not bear a single moment longer having to see this abomination rewrite all that is and was! I ran up to him in my rage, and placed my hands on his head to wrest control of his device from him, force-on-force! I battled The Unmaker mind-to-mind, trying to force the true history of everything back into its rightful place... but for my promising start, it was beginning to go wrong. I could feel him pushing back, figuring me out, where to poke and prod in my technique, my offense, my defense... I was stalwart as hell, but he was making more progress on me than I was on him... I knew what was inevitable.

At the edge of the Dyson Shield, the Haji-Son Combined Armada gathered, and the Redarian Interplanetary Battlefleet was prepared to meet them. All that separated the two armies was that shield.

"They're hailing us, Arch-Militant" the helmsman of the *Spear of The Velani* informed Jarrek, to which he nodded, telling him to patch the message through.

"I was wondering who you would choose as your... personal vessel," Jarrek greeted disdainfully, knowing full well who was puppeting Exemplar Kendro-Dalinor.

"Arch-Militant Wöllschlager." The Haji-Son Exemplar returned the greeting from the *Void Pillar,* the flagship of the Combined Armada. But The Unmaker's will spoke now through the moral leader of the four species that were part of the Haji-Son family. "The word was not as quick to travel as I'd have liked, but travel all the same it did."

"And what word is that, pray tell?" Jarrek asked.

"I thought stalling was beneath you, Arch-Militant."

"I'm not stalling, you are!"

But Jarrek was very much stalling, and maybe distracting Kendro-Dalinor with a ridiculous contradictory argument could do the trick. The Exemplar was having none of it, however.

"My ships will head to Aldin, they will deal with the Way Gate, and he who has constructed it. The only thing that remains is to find out if I have to tear through this shield and your armada to do it."

Several ships of Taigron make warped in behind the Haji-Son fleet. The Unmaker was now beginning to show his power, his ability to bring a whole universe under his command.

"Exemplar, I know that it's The Unmaker speaking through your mouth and acting through your body, and that's why I want nothing more than to not fight you. Once Radien deals with the son of a bitch, my plan is to step onto the bridge of your ship and give you a damn hug, old friend. That's why I won't risk destroying my ships or yours, since I know none of your pilots would want to fight mine on any other day. That said... I have more ways to make it hell for you to get to Aldin than cannons and missiles. I command the combined defensive capabilities of the entire Velani Array, and it is my express intent to make that your problem."

Jarrek pressed a button on his console and issued his command to the fleet. "Fire them now!"

Every ship that was on the Velani side of the Dyson Shield fired modified payloads at the barrier, by way of cannon and missile alike, whose raw energetic charges now suddenly bolstered the integrity of the shield instead of tearing it asunder, like the armaments of the Haji-Son fleet attempted. After the initial volley, the Redarian ships broke off and scattered, leaving behind additional EMP mines and Vortex Emulators that if any hostile ship collided with them, they would be shut down almost completely in the case of the EMP mines. As for the Vortex Emulators, the ships that eagerly broke through the Dyson Shield found themselves caught in a secondary vacuum that drained entire engine cores just to break free of. The Subspace Vacuole Generators were similar, yanking away the ability for ships to simply warp away from the fray.

With Micah and Veralis both aboard the *Spear of The Velani* to monitor the enemy fleet's progress, and assign defensive measures accordingly, everyone was pretty occupied. So much so, that if it weren't for the fact that someone else yelled out that there was an incoming message from Laksor, none of them would have noticed.

"This the Spear," Jarrek acknowledged to Jaden, who was initiating the transmission.

"The Way Gate on Aldin's been powered up. I only just noticed it, and it's likely *been* powered up for some time now."

"So why didn't Radien tell us? What the hell is he waiting for?!" Jarrek growled.

"This is Radien we're talking about!" Veralis quickly reminded. "He went in on his own!"

Miles and the Effigy still sat across from each other at that familiar table as he sighed heavily.

"And now we're here, back where you and I started this conversation, Effigy," Miles repeated. "As I stretch these last few moments of mine to hours, and I know what I can do. There is still a way to defeat The Unmaker, and I think it's all I've got left."

Miles's voice was heavy as he told the Effigy his plan. "I can stop fighting him, and start fighting myself. Convert my body into energy, overload him, destroy him utterly. I'd sacrifice myself to break The Unmaker's stranglehold on all creation, and it's the best way to go I can think of, honestly.

Just me and The Unmaker, we'd be the only casualties of this final battle, and that's perfectly fine by me."

The Effigy continued to listen.

"I don't fear death. I never have. Which is why my imminent end is not why I'm so hesitant to do what must be done. It's you, Effigy. It's what will happen to you once I'm gone. You're a creation of my mind, a being who only exists to me, and... and the universe loses you, a creature so wise, so strong, so much so that he's never even had to say a word in all the years I've known him... You'd fade. Because no one but me knows you, and I'm about to die. You're both too good for this universe, and too good to let disappear with no one having known your name."

The Effigy still listened, as Miles drew a few tired breaths, speaking what felt like confessions to him.

Miles's six closest allies had assembled in front of the Way Gate to the Field of Unreality. Veralis, Arakai, Micah, Jarrek, Miirkae and Dorg all made their mental preparations, wondering just what awaited them inside.

After stepping through, the city that Miles walked through had become no larger than the few blocks surrounding the pyramid, and the few dozen remaining simulacrums that surrounded it, waiting their turn to disappear.

"Who are they?" Dorg asked.

"My guess is people for The Unmaker to play around with. I suppose fake reality stopped being as satisfying," Miirkae growled.

Arakai shook his head in doubt. "If that were the case, why are there city blocks here for them to live in, rather than cages?"

Veralis was the one who bothered to walk up and ask.

"You're from the same reality as Creator, and the other that came by," one of the denizens quickly discerned. "He went into the pyramid to do what needs to be done. I just hope you're here to help him..."

"You do know that—" Arakai started, and was quickly cut off by the denizen confirming his awareness that he, and everyone else in the simulation would cease to exist when The Unmaker was destroyed.

"At first, our awareness of the nature of our existence did not bother us. It was fine, that we had form and voice by Creator's will alone. That stopped being the case once we began to fade, because his will was ceasing to be our continued existence."

As he looked around and saw that two more had vanished, he sighed. "We're tired of waiting. At this point, what you promise is solace that we won't die meaninglessly."

The group cautiously walked into the pyramid, prepared for battle. But they saw eerie emptiness, and harrowing silence. Except Miirkae, though. One of his ears twitched.

"What do you hear, *Ku-la nai*?" Dorg quickly asked.

"Radien. He's fighting... but not in the normal sense. And whatever sense that is, he's struggling."

The group followed the keen-eared Hykentiu towards the central apex, and Veralis gasped as she saw the spectacle of Miles locked in mental combat with The Unmaker. Micah and Jarrek both looked upon the projections of history that The Unmaker had altered, and the ones Miles was fighting to restore.

"Radien?" Veralis quietly said as she approached the man standing still with his hands pressed against The Unmaker's head. Sheathing her axes, she managed to stop herself from placing a hand on his shoulder, so as to not risk whatever side effects might come of interfering.

"He's fighting hard, and valiantly," Micah commented as she held a scanner. "But he's tiring. I don't even think The Unmaker is going to beat Radien by outfighting or outclassing him. The way it's going..."

"Miles Radien is about to literally die fighting," Veralis finished. "Fighting so hard and for so long, he forgets to do anything else... even breathe."

Miles was ready now. There was only one last thing to tell this vision of the kind of person he wished he could have been, and then he would be at peace.

"You're everything I'd be if I could be anyone, Effigy... If I could be like you, even just a shadow of the being you are... That would be my greatest victory of all."

To Miles's horror, the Effigy flickered and distorted in this final space of his mind, and he shot up from his chair as the visage of his stronger self was replaced with The Unmaker, staring right at him.

"What the hell?! Does your wickedness and dishonor know no bounds?!"

"Hell," the ancient Dragon said. "Realm of the Dark

Six and all their armies. I am intimately familiar."

Miles charged forward in his mind's space and unleashed a vicious kick on the defiler of the Effigy, who though thrown to the ground by the force, seemed unharmed overall, standing back up with casual demeanor.

"Thinking about hurting me doesn't hurt me. But I thought we could at least speak before one or both of us dies," The Unmaker gruffed.

"I have nothing to say to you, Unmaker."

"Please, I am Melaqros."

Miles was shocked. He knew what that name meant now, and The Unmaker was using it for himself? Despite the immense taboo it would be to misuse this name, Miles couldn't help but figure that it wasn't beyond The Unmaker to do it.

"I am not oblivious to the ways of the stars," The Unmaker continued. "Someone has risen against me with startling effectiveness. Not just that, but someone from a backwater planet home to a species addicted to corruption. But here you are, in defiance of your race's primal nature."

"Oh, cut it the fuck out already, *I get it already!* Humans are *shit!* I've known that forever, and I've known that always!" Miles suddenly spat. "If there was ever a species of inherent and objective evil to rival that of the Humans, it's the Demons, but to be honest, Demons are a lot more honorable! At least you know what you're getting into when it comes to Demons, but *Humans,* no, *Humans* have to be such fucking deceitful, dishonorable *pricks* about it!"

The Unmaker prepared to say his next part, but Miles

interrupted before it even began, seething with rage at how he had mentioned the Humans, and so gravely insulted Miles by calling him one. "Don't even start with me, I already *fucking* agree! Humans are the gods-damned worst, I want nothing more than that lot to end! They love evil, their favorite taste is boot leather, they are the worst kind of *Khaehnhaalet, Fiir-taefuol Drushainen Vohaienarr Rahkaes Soldaikrüss!*"

It was as if Miles had made these words up on their own to dishonor the Human species more severely than any language he knew allowed. The guttural curses that he spewed, however, were of the ancient Draconian language that The Unmaker spoke naturally. There existed no words to translate just what Miles had said. There was nothing in any Human language that could even begin to describe just what fiery insults Miles Radien called the Humans, titles they deserved beyond any other.

"Does that fucking do it for you?!" Miles then shouted at his foe. "Does that gods-damned get it into your *fucking* head that I agree with you that the Humans should *fucking die?!* Have I yet, *Paavrainn?!*"

The Unmaker simply looked at Miles, just standing there, genuinely startled at how much the man in front of him had just viciously cursed his own species, and his rage slowly turned to weary sighs, and if not for fatigue, a chuckle might have followed, but it couldn't be mustered. "Congratulations, man. Here I thought that part of me was finally at rest. I thought that tired old me had found peace in his escape. But you got it to come back out. You and your hundred-year siege on reality itself."

The Unmaker stood there, shocked and without words. This person had just snapped at him with the kind of fury that only a kind person could bring to bear when you finally wore out their patience.

"This last century, Unmaker, I've had to learn that friend after friend has sided with you and against me. I know I stand alone, it's the oldest truth. But it's a tired one, one that I had dared to hope might change when I finally escaped Earth. And now suddenly here you came, to take it all away. But isn't that just my luck?"

Miles then leaned against a wall, thudding the back of his head on it with fatigue. "I've gotten so clever at avoiding your forces, I figured out so many damn ways to make sure I didn't fall to you. I thought of a million remedies if I shook in your wake, I thought of a million ways to make sure the mission could continue if I failed. I've got over a dozen different plans on how my friends should destroy me if I found myself under your yoke, and even more for in case *they* were to betray! I'm so *fucking* clever, and I'm so *fucking tired* of being so clever all the time... I cannot deny what you've taught me, all the ways you have made sure I will be forever stalwart. I cannot deny that in learning how to survive you, I've learned how to survive everyone. But I've learned it all against my will."

The two stood there in silence as The Unmaker wondered just what to say. In and out did he then breathe before he spoke at last. "If you should not only defeat me, but survive doing so, seek the Perawls of Dor-Val-Der."

“The Perawls? The guardians of the Great Forbidden Weapons? Do not seek to deceive me!” Miles’s confusion was now more than ever. Why was The Unmaker helping him?

“Dor-Val-Der itself has not become mine to command, or I’d be telling you myself what you need to know from Perawl Moreis.”

“Why are you telling me this?! What does this deception do for you other than just stall?!”

“It may be hard to believe, but my greater interest is in the fate of the universe. And if I fall, *someone’s* got to have a plan for the coming storm.”

The two stood in silence once again, before The Unmaker spoke once more, now with a tone of solemnity, and his eyes drifting away from Miles’s contact, now staring contemplative into the distance. “Someone like you doesn’t just happen one day... I’ve read the stories and heard the tales of people like you, and those people... I’d bet that ever since you took on The Aura, you’ve rarely bothered to sleep. I doubt you’ve rested a single moonrise since I began my work proper. And I wonder how many more will there be before one night, one great and terrible night... you will find yourself counting them all?”

*“Begone, Unmaker!”* Miles shouted, slamming his fist into the ground and pulsing a great wave of energy though this space of his own, this space of his mind. The Unmaker’s image distorted and flickered, before vanishing entirely.

And now Miles Radien stood alone. At the end of the line, with one last choice to make, Miles Radien stood alone one last time, breathing heavily, exhausted and weary.

"What do I do?" He wondered aloud.

From behind him, Miles heard something shuffling about. He whipped around, ready to fight, but just saw the Effigy once again, holding his cup of mead and looking into it.

Then, something impossible happened. The Effigy rose the cup to his lips, and drained it, resolutely slamming it onto the counter he leaned against, as he spoke the only three words Miles ever needed to hear, in a voice the man recognized as his own.

"Claim your victory."

Miles's eyes shot open back in the chamber he once thought was his tomb, where he would make his final stand, but that he now saw and understood as where he would make his apotheosis. And somehow, his friends had followed him. They were in the room, Veralis, Micah, Arakai, Jarrek, even Miirkae and Dorg. New images drew themselves upon the walls, depictions no one had ever seen before, because they were not history.

"Of course..." Veralis said as her dread was replaced with hope. "Just how many worlds danced in your head, Radien? How powerful is your mind's eye, that you could create a whole new face for yourself and who you would be, that you would be proud to call your own?"

Jarrek stood up and looked upon what Miles showed them all. And not just the five friends in the room, no—What Miles was showing *everyone*, across all the planets and all the moons, every ship, every station, every satellite was now beholding Miles Radien's dreams, and his wildest fantasies of saving them all. Leading the charge was none other than the

Effigy, his left hand holding the Borfblade high as the new golden dawn rose for all creation, and all its peoples.

"He's not showing them what was..." Miirkae said in awe. "He's showing them what could be! A promise, of a universe that stands tall, that stands strong..."

"The Unmaker can't touch them! He had no part in these memories because they were never experienced, they were *created!*" Micah added. "He can't help but tell everyone what Radien's promising them, the promise of a universe without The Unmaker!"

"A universe defended!" Veralis finished with resolute strength, and Miles looked into her eyes as The Unmaker seethed and writhed upon his throne of lies. "Radien... I know you don't need me to tell you this... but end his madness!"

Miles cracked a smirk as he nodded to Veralis, leaning to The Unmaker's ear and whispering the last words that would be on his foe's mind as it faded to black:

"You are defeated!"

A final surge of power, and The Unmaker was utterly destroyed in a great flash of light.

The city around them crumbled, as its creator was no longer there to hold its existence, and soon the Field of Unreality was an endless plain of empty canvas, save for the chair and devices of the ill-fated Unmaker, a few scattered desks with tattered manuscripts and volumes, likely what little he had brought over from the physical universe before remaining in the Field of Unreality.

"I guess he just kinda... made himself a world to live in when he got here so he wouldn't go mad,"

Jarrek commented.

A few snarky remarks from the others like "Yeah, and that sure worked out" and similar were what Miles and Veralis heard as the other five exited via the Way Gate. Miles was a little jittery, he was feeling quite the rush after a moment like that.

Suddenly, he threw his arm forward and blasted away a great explosion of the raw power of The Aura, and looked over to Veralis, who just stood there.

"Just letting off a bit of steam, that was a hell of a rush! Not to mention I think I absorbed all The Unmaker's own power, and I gotta disperse that a bit—"

He then blasted away again, thankful that he wasn't on an actual planet that would've had something he might hit. "He was a powerful guy, that's for sure..."

"Radien, what's—" Veralis said as he fired off again, a slight desperation in both his movements and his voice.

"I'll be fine. I have to be. I can make this work!" Miles stammered, firing off again and again, using all his might to disperse all the energy he had taken in.

"But... The Unmaker was destroyed! His power would've just dispersed with the rest of the matter that made up his body, right?" Veralis said, as confused as Miles was growing desperate.

Miles's shoulders fell as his eyes became weary and sorrowful, like he just heard the one bad news in all creation that he never wanted to. "I just... I... oh gods, if only."

Veralis was suddenly overcome with sorrow herself, but she didn't quite know why. She was picking it up from

Miles, her Psionic Empathy knew that he felt as though he just heard he was about to die. And as far as Miles knew, he just heard that.

"The Humans are a young species," Miles started, with great and trained effort to conceal the physical pain he was enduring holding his body together. "I'm the first one to ever wield The Aura, I'm from a planet that had no Fonts... was it only a matter of time?"

"Radien, what is it? What's happening to you?!" Veralis approached, but Miles held his arm out to stop her.

"For all The Aura has given me, my physical body... can't take it much longer, it seems. First-generation Aura Warrior of the Humans, looks like the maximum lifespan is... seven hundred years about... argh!"

In that instant, she figured it out. Miles's very cells were starting to destabilize, unable to contain the foreign entity that was The Aura any longer. With the Humans never having known Cosmic Power, their forms wouldn't be able to sustain it forever. "There has to be something," Veralis offered. "I can—"

"No, Veralis!" Miles shouted, holding his arm out again, to a crackling wall of energy that quickly went unstable and fizzled out. "The only way you're saving me is by taking it away, and I refuse! I can't go back to a frail and mortal body, even if refusing to kills me... There's nothing you can offer in its stead, nothing you or anyone can do that would console me after losing all this... I choose to die whole, Veralis. I will not live broken."

Veralis wasn't sure which direction to step in. Away, to

let her friend die? Towards, and defy his wishes? Miles conjured an orb in his hand, ready to defend himself. But the orb was... malformed. It crackled and distorted in its own instability.

"I don't want to fight you, Veralis. But I will if that's what I must do!" Miles said, staunchly refusing to shed a tear. It was working, too. Though his grief was clear, his eyes didn't even water from the sheer force of his will alone. "I make my choice, to die whole. These were my best years, and I will be at peace, knowing I got to have them..."

Miles's body began to glow strands of bright gold and blue power, The Aura radiating from him as he could barely hold himself together. "I saw those worlds, the ones I dreamed of, and I saved them! Just as I had dreamed of... and... and..."

He then turned back towards Veralis, his eyes no longer tired, but calm, even peaceful. "...I got to meet you. I met and made my friends, the friends I've been honored to call my allies! Arakai, Jarrek, Micah, Miirkae, Dorg... And all the others! Xenidar on Turazin, Kyrana and Iraine on Bol'Drakkin... I even remember the name of that Loriken I sparred with on Orvitaire now... Her name was Nirial..."

As much as Miles understood that Veralis was fighting back tears of her own, he couldn't actually see whether or not she was succeeding over the almost blinding glow of his own body radiating away as energy. "My life's been the dream I dreamed... but even then, I always knew someday I'd have to wake up..."

He closed his eyes, and with a few final deep breaths,

Miles Radien let go. With no more strength to spare, his body erupted in raw power, as if the universe itself was being born of his fire. And the yell that he let loose, it seethed with the rage that he despised to leave his friends and this whole universe behind, but beneath it there was still that serenity, that he lived a life so much more fulfilling than he could've ever dared to hope for.

The voice faded and trailed off in the steady stream of golden and azure energy that filled this pocket of the Field of Unreality, and Veralis had needed to take several further steps back to avoid being blinded by the sheer light alone.

When it was finally safe to look back, the light still was dying down. The energy had yet to fully dissipate, and when she turned back to where the Human once stood, there was no Human standing there, not anymore.

Instead, there stood Miles Sorvenjar Radien, Death World Vulpian!

*"Radien!!"* Veralis called out as she rushed over, and he gasped as he realized just what had happened, that he was still alive! Not only was he still alive, he *was* the Effigy! He had taken the form of the stronger and wiser being that had been in his mind for so long, that he wished he could be!

"Veralis!" Radien exclaimed as she grabbed him and held him tight, her arms wrapped around his shoulders as his didn't really know where to go, for lack of experience being this close to anyone. "It let me stay! The Aura let me stay!"

Radien was quivering with joy, his breath rapid and relieved as Veralis still held onto him. His hands were just extended out past her, held in closed fists as he still tried to comprehend that he was alive, that he was a Death World Vulpian, that he was the Effigy.

"All that I thought I knew that told me I was dying... and I realize now, the Aura Prism knew something else from the start."

Slowly raising his left hand towards her, Veralis nodded as he then placed it on her cheek to show her just what he was remembering, of that day on Cynofrax, where he first met the Aura Prism, where he first was shown and took the gift of The Aura.

*"...You are only Human in body, Miles. You heart, your mind, your very soul... They belong to another race. Which exactly, I cannot say. Only you will be able to, in time. But beyond any doubt, I can guarantee you, not by destiny, but simply by what I know of the universe... You will be far, far greater than a Human could ever dream of being. Because even your dreams aren't Human. They're anyone else, from anywhere else."*

*"I owe you a debt I can never repay."*

*"Your deeds will decide that. You may be immortal, but you are not invincible. You can still die, but it would practically have to be by your own will."*

Then came the words, the truth that the Aura Prism knew all along, that Radien only just now truly realize what they meant. *"Your form will adjust to your power."*

He rested his head against Veralis's shoulder as she chuckled and commented on how the Prism was an entity of mysterious deliberation, who always meant every word, even if no one else really knew it yet. But Radien was just glad, and utterly unable to keep secret the joy and relief beyond all imagining that he didn't have to leave this universe behind. He didn't have to leave anyone behind. The dream was no dream, and there was nothing to wake up from.

The Field of Unreality now only had scattered devices that The Unmaker had brought from the universe at first, that he didn't want to have to rebuild. That and the many personal diaries and logs. Radien studied the volumes, as all the other machines had dissipated in The Unmaker's absence. Veralis walked up to him.

"Well, now I know why he did it. I sure don't agree that it was the right course of action, but I do know what his logic was, and I can comprehend how he got there," Radien said, slapping the book back onto the table.

"The personal musings and conclusions of Arigen Concarius…" Veralis observed of the title.

"That was his name," Radien stated. "The Unmaker was none other than Arigen Concarius, the guy who was seeking that save-state universe all those eons ago."

Radien flipped through a few of the other volumes on the table, his eyes just as quickly reading, scanning, and learning the information with The Aura's eidetic memory. "When he discovered this place, the Field of Unreality, he decided to use it as a base, a staging ground to do what no one else had even thought of doing: Spy on Hell. He went to the Burning Hells, infiltrating and learning about Demons. These books, this knowledge… it's more than anyone has ever gathered on Demons, combined. The different kinds of demons, their hierarchies and ranks, the structures of their societies… it's… well, it's everything."

Veralis paged through one of the books that Radien had just put down, which contained detailed drawings of different breeds of Demons, and also a breakdown on their written language.

"With the Field of Unreality, he had the perfect hiding spot. The Demons couldn't track him to here, and we sure as hell couldn't either. So he just kept going back and forth, kept learning, until the day he found out what made him realize, that the only way to keep the universe safe was to make it unquestioningly united, with him, the guy who knew all there was to know about Demons as the commander of all the universe and its armies."

"If he were the hero of every story, no one would question that he knew what to do," Veralis concluded as Radien nodded. "Talk about the Mortus Paradox…"

The Mortus Paradox, being a term to describe a particular kind of twisted mind's motivation, derived from the principle of '*Any profession, cause, or goal, if taken to enough of an extreme in its interpretation, can arrive at the conclusion that eliminating all life is the optimal path.*' Essentially, the sort of madman's motivation that if a doctor's purpose is to heal the sick, and the dead cannot get sick, thus the solution is that killing everyone kills disease.

Mortus Paradox was simply the term given to this oddly specific yet prevalent way of thinking that often motivated villains of massive grandeur. But in this case, Arigen Concarius, The Unmaker, intended to become the hero of every story, so that no one would hesitate to believe his judgment was correct, and the universe would be under his command.

"According to these, as he gathered intelligence, and amassed all the information he did, his original plan was to just return to the universe once he felt satisfied with what he had learned," Radien continued. "But then he learned something else, something that shook him to the core, so much so that he believed there wasn't time to tell his story. Couldn't risk the delays that skepticism and scrutiny would bring."

With a sigh, Radien set the last of the journals back onto the desk. "The Dark Six have returned to Hell."

Veralis didn't flinch physically, but it was like her soul did instead. "They've escaped from *Unapasakl-Aura Käynenrel?"*

The name of the prison dimension that the Dark Six were confined to after the end of the First War for Reality, it roughly translated as 'Eternally power-destroying place,' but the more common name for it was 'Doomrealm.'

"It was a long time coming, but even the Old Cynofraxians knew that it wasn't a permanent solution, that prison dimension," Radien said, nodding solemnly. "But yes... the Dark Six have returned to their home, to marshal all of their forces, and prepare for the final push. And at the end of it all, The Oldest War will be over. Either because we win... or because they do."

The two simply stood over the desk, and the journals of Arigen Concarius. "I'm going to take these to Xenidar, and make sure he gets them into the hands of... well, everyone," Radien then said. "As much as The Unmaker did in his assassination attempt on history itself, this is still invaluable information on the Demons and their masters."

Veralis nodded as he gathered the books. "Strange..." He then commented. "As much dread as I have for this oncoming doom, I feel an overwhelming calm, as if... as if this is exactly what I've been preparing for. All I am, all I know, all I believe... leading to this. Like the universe has been training me, but not. I know the universe does not train people, but I feel as though I am trained for the universe."

"To defend it," Veralis realized. "Universal Defender... it's you, isn't it? You're the tenth Defender, aren't you?" Her expression wasn't one of shock, but a more quiet satisfaction, for all the pieces falling into place.

"I've heard of that title before," Miles remarked as he telekinetically carried the books through the Way Gate, and Veralis followed him back to Aldin Moon. "Even did some research on the people who've had it. And I'm not sure if I've got any right to be claiming that lofty of an honor."

"That's generally how they worked," Veralis remarked. "Historically, the Defenders never boasted themselves that, or strove for the title, or petitioned a vote. They just... as people, that's what they found purpose in. Making things right, solving problems, helping out."

"Wouldn't that be the life." Radien chuckled.

"Precisely."

Radien then realized that Veralis was being serious. She really did believe that he was the tenth Defender. This confused him greatly, especially the idea that someone was actively believing in him to any capacity. "I, uh..."

His words trailed off as he realized he didn't have any, and so he just shrugged with that fact.

"Well, you don't have to know. Not today," Veralis assured, putting a hand on his shoulder, to an inquisitive look from the now-Death World Vulpian. "Right now, I think we both need a bit of revelry. The universe is rid of The Unmaker, and we have you to thank for that!"

Radien nodded, some victory drinks definitely would hit the spot. They were had at the Warrior's Gate, back on Raon-Arashal. The buzz was definitely on about Radien's new, more true-to-soul body. Still the same five-foot-seven stocky build, but now in that Vulpine shape and definition. The muscles on his arms were a bit denser and more defined, not to mention the fur coat. He'd probably have to hang up that old stone grey jacket of his, since he wouldn't exactly need it anymore. A pattern of sand-like shades, and the distinct shape across his shoulders and back in a soft bronze, it looked like a sword coming from the back of his head to about the middle of his tail, which he was already getting quite used to having, to his surprise. He had initially thought it would take a few days, but Radien certainly seemed a natural at sporting a healthy tail. His eyes had also changed color, too. The greyish blue was replaced with a strong green, and overall, it fit him. He definitely felt as though it was a form that suited him.

Of course, nobody was disputing that, and his friends and comrades certainly thought it worked, too. Several times did Radien have to playfully smack away a slowly encroaching

Jarrek hand that was coming in to try to pat him, as well as plenty of 'Maybe later' type banter.

Folk songs of Raon-Arashal and of Redaria were being sung in the Warrior's Gate as the universe celebrated the end of The Unmaker, as food, drink and merriment all were exchanged.

*Pir dolgelse sol thej, pir dolgelse sol thej!*
*Pir jaltai-nah pir iklae, djozernaaverash toulth sol kallej!*
*Viir duunraeynar torval'e krae, dwerai thej kel yagitay!*
*Jasaln givol sol hol-nah orgaen, pir dolgelse sol thej!*
*With doom we come, with doom we come!*
*With sword and with spear,*
*to destroy our enemies with our allies!*
*Fight the fear for honor's sake,*
*finally bring forth victory!*
*On mountains of virtue we stand and shout,*
*with doom we come!*

Naturally, the song only worked from a syllabic standpoint when actually sung in the Death World Vulpian language. It was but one of many people were spontaneously belting out in the celebrations.

When Radien went out onto a balcony to take a quick breather, he couldn't help but remember how it all began. So suddenly, and so long ago. Everything was happening all at once, and that had only become more clear as he researched and learned about that day, and the other powers at play in that fateful hour.

The currents of The Aura were strong in Raon-Arashal, and Radien's attunement to the power made him realize that he wasn't alone on this balcony. So he closed his eyes, and let himself enter a blank space in his mind where he and this power could meet face-to-face.

"No way..." Were the first words he said, as a bronze-scaled Bol'Drakkin Draconian stood in front of him.

"You've done well for yourself," he said, but in a slightly different voice than Radien remembered. Then again, it was probably the Melaqros's normal voice, rather than the one being spoken under pressure.

"I still don't know your name," Radien admitted.

"Talgoron," The Dragon introduced, admittedly almost seven centuries late. "Talgoron, the Brighttaloned, of the Kasven Line."

"Kasven line... of course, that's how you had the Aura Runner." Only one of the Defenders ever had descendants: Ahron Kasven, the first of the line, who built the Archaeotech ship of myth himself. Passed down from descendant to descendant, the Dragons of the Kasven Line were the keepers of the Aura Runner, until it came to Radien's hands. "That's one of my two questions answered, then."

Talgoron tilted his head with curiosity before Radien asked that second question.

"How?" he said simply. "Earth's too... *Earth* for you to have just stumbled on it, and yet..."

"You know how the Prism sometimes will say something that you find out later had a much deeper, truer meaning than what you thought it did at that moment?" Talgoron responded, to a hearty nod and chuckle from Radien. "And of course, the Prism knew that was what they meant the whole time, it just took you that long to figure it out... I often spent time wandering the stars in the Aura Runner, seeing if there was something I could fix, someone I could aid. One day, the Aura Prism tells me, to go to a seemingly backwater sector, in a spiral galaxy some of its locals called the Milky Way, to a particular solar system... *'And you will find a soul in search of answers.'"*

"Sounds like the kind of thing the Prism would say."

"Indeed it was. So I warped my way over there, and found to my horror a great emptiness where The Aura should have been. A desert in space, a whole solar system where there was no Psionic power. There was... well, to put it plainly, there was no magic, only a dreadful and ominous shadow that drained the universe's lifeblood from itself in this place. And yet, in this desert, there was an oasis. A Font that had almost ripped itself into existence out of defiance, and that's where the soul surely was. Radiating pure cosmic power, like he would be the one to force color to return to a cold, grey world, because no one else was."

Radien just stood there as he listened. He heard those words before, a long time ago, but back then they were barely rushed out sputters before death, and only a faint hope that he could stumble onto the right path from there. Most likely, if given the time, Talgoron would've been saying all this instead.

"They were Dark Six servants, the ones who fired that shot," Radien said. "As soon as the Aura Runner came within ten million miles of Earth, they knew and started laying their trap. They'd found my beacon too, they just figured no one else would."

Talgoron nodded.

"And in killing you so quickly, they could score a craft that had been their nemesis once, whose name had lived in infamy within the Hells for so long. Even now, I'm still learning new things about that day, what powers were setting plans in motion," Radien continued. "The last seven hundred years have been a damn whirlwind, with barely any time for me to catch my footing. I feel like I've been winging it for seven centuries, despite how long of a time that is."

Talgoron continued to listen as Radien seemed on the verge of getting his bearings for the first time in… well, likely his whole life.

"I've just been… reacting, doing the best I can as everything suddenly throws itself at me. I still hardly understand what it means to exist in such a vast universe, much less… what it means to truly be Radien."

"Seven hundred years is only a long time for someone who comes from a species that rarely lives beyond a hundred," Talgoron admitted. "With The Aura at your side, and the allies you've already made, I have full confidence that you will assert yourself as the Radien you wish the worlds to know."

"Oh, don't flatter," Radien quickly cut in. "But… for you, I will endeavor. Talgoron, I owe you a debt I can never repay. You saved me from Earth. If not for you… well, you know damn well how much wouldn't have ever come to pass."

"Then there is someone you can repay that debt to,"

Talgoron informed as Radien perked up. "Someone who has yet to know just where they come from, who could certainly stand to find out."

The vision of Talgoron began to fade as the veil between mortal reality and the beyond re-asserted itself. Neither he nor Radien felt the need to say anything more, just to stand tall and resolute in the parting of the ways. Back on the balcony, Radien's eyes opened, and he looked down on his body, a grin creeping across his face that he was a Death World Vulpian as he walked back into the Warrior's Gate to continue the festivities.

A few days later on the planet of Bol'Drakkin, Radien found the budding artificer and tinkerer he was looking for.

"Crimzin, the Brightminded?" Radien called to him as the red-scaled Dragon looked over, lifting up his protective glasses to reveal the regular glasses underneath.

"Yes?" He answered.

Radien looked at the item Crimzin was working on enchanting. "That's... actually really impressive, how long have you been studying artificing for?"

"About... three ASC now, I think."

"That's really good for only three ASC, normally it takes a good five or six to get to that point."

Radien was telling the truth. Crimzin seemed to have a knack for the arcane. No wonder he had that title on his name, Brightminded. "Torvaltyne Bastion still needs a Resident Artificer, there would be a place for you on Raon-Arashal if you wanted it."

Crimzin scoffed with a slight disbelief. "Really? And

what's stopping you from recruiting someone exponentially more qualified?"

"The fact that I don't recruit the best. I recruit the people who can become the best, and I make sure they've got the tools, the means, and the chance," Radien responded.

"Hell, I've got nothing worth staying here for. Though transport might be a bit of an issue, since—"

"Dude, I run the dang fort. You think I can't order one of my pilots to get you there? Besides, we'll take my ship anyway, once you're ready."

Crimzin grabbed a few items off the Artificer's table, then rummaged about in his desk, putting some personal effects and notebooks into a backpack that he had managed to tie to a pocket dimension. It was no small feat for someone who'd only been studying artificing for three ASC to successfully make a bag of holding. "All right, then," he eventually said, with his belongings ready.

Radien brought Crimzin into the Aura Runner, setting the course for Raon-Arashal.

"It feels..." Crimzin started.

"Familiar?" Radien asked.

"No... just..." Crimzin said as he walked around the ship, studying its interior and trying to find the word he was looking for. "It feels like this ship knows me, even though I don't know it."

Radien turned around to tell Crimzin the story of Talgoron, the Brighttaloned. "You're not as wrong as you might think."

# GLOSSARY OF SPECIES

**Ascendant** – "Ascendant" is an umbrella term for any mechanical creature that has attained sentience, thus, 'ascended' into the realm of the thinking and reasoning. If a formerly non-sentient robot were to learn how to think for itself and be its own being, they would immediately be recognized as a sentient creature, with all the rights and responsibilities thereof. Ascendant come in hundreds, if not thousands of variants, but the most common types are the tall, lizard-like 'Shiar Pattern' Ascendant, and the slightly more furred, and often shorter in stature 'Neo-Proto Pattern' Ascendant. Both utilize pixel-display visors on their heads to convey facial expression and emotions, as well as replaceable energy cores that last for up to thousands of years at a time, allowing most Ascendant to live for as long as they wish.

**Corvuseine** – The corvid species from !leysa, though not endangered by any means, more or less 'happen to be not too common' in the grand scheme of species. They are also just as enigmatic by happenstance over desire to be so, and can often seem hard to approach. But this is not usually the case, and Corvuseine are rarely shy from meeting new people, just as long as they refrain from commenting about how seldom they see Corvuseine. Their home planet of !leysa is renowned for playing host to some of the most prestigious culinary schools in the universe, as well as the most respected playwrights.

**Draconians** – There are many different types of Dragon species across the universe, three major "Genetic Castes." and dozens of other variants that are still considered to be just as much Dragons as any other kind. The major variants of Dragon are the Bol'Drakkin Genetic Caste, hailing from the titular world of Bol'Drakkin in the Nashira Strand solar system, the Nuvenr from Teyn-Var-Wolk, and the Skevalidur, whose origin planet is disputed. Even Skevalidur historians can't seem to glean much more than "Well, we just kinda... happened one day and nobody minded more Dragons out and about, so...." to quote Razh Terisi, one such Skevalidur historian. Bol'Drakkin Dragons are generally more resemblant of the 'Western Dragon' type, while Nuvenr Dragons are decidedly more akin to the 'Eastern Dragons' of myth. It is believed that the myths of Dragons on Earth originated from crashed exploration ships from either species, a surprisingly not uncommon phenomenon in the universe.

**Felinian** – There used to be three major Felinians, the Elurian, the Nuberi, and the Aliken Sor. Only the Nuberi and Aliken Sor exist today, as the Elurians were rendered extinct after the corruption of Caltoran, a genocide that countless still mourn across the universe. The Aliken Sor are the more 'traditional' feline type, but that has only ever been said by ignorant Humans that have only ever seen house cats in their lifetimes, while the Nuberi are closer to the Lynx in appearance. The main difference between the Aliken Sor and Nuberi in demeanor is that while the Aliken Sor generally strive for a more refined and restrained lifestyle, the Nuberi have no such drive for order and organization, which has resulted in metaphors like "Put a red dot on a wall, and both Aliken Sor and Nuberi will charge for it. But only the Nuberi would forget that they're the one holding the laser pointer."

**Hajikahl** – Though the Hajivakk, Hajitorr and Hajinehr are all feline Haji-Son, the Hajikahl are the exception, being a canine species with a natural affinity for pyrokinesis and other fire-related things. Hajikahl have an internal body temperature high enough for them to be a radiating source of heat, often to the gratitude of cold-blooded species such as Dragons or Varok-Torividan. Though the Hajitorr are the more laid-back Haji-Son, the Hajikahl are the single most adaptable, seemingly always able to go with whatever flow any situation has. To quote Miles Radien on the subject of the Hajikahl, "I'd call their demeanor like a river, but then that river would have to be on fire. Imagine a river that didn't mind being on fire, I guess."

**Hajinehr** – Of the four Haji-Son species that hail from the Nashira Strand solar system, the Hajinehr are the single most adept sneaks of them all, much like the panthers they resemble. Though the image of stealth and thievery is a bit of a rude stereotype to associate with the Hajinehr, it does remain the case that they are very, very good at it, sometimes to their own chagrin. A common lament from Hajinehr Masters of Shadow is "Why am I so good at stealth? I wanted to be good at anything else!"

**Hajitorr** – If the Hajinehr are akin to panthers, and the Hajivakk are akin to snow leopards, then the Hajitorr are akin to cheetahs. Another of the four Haji-Son species, Hajitorr are almost the polar opposite of the Hajivakk in general demeanor, being much more laid-back, and preferring hotter climates. Though all feline species share a vulnerability for lounging in spaces that perfectly fit the size of their bodies, Hajitorr are decidedly more susceptible to 'Box-sitting addiction"

**Hajivakk** – One of the four Haji-Son species, the leopard-like Hajivakk often prefer colder climates, thus their major population centers on Mjarfus and Homphalion, though their Capitol World is actually Caren'Das. The Hajivakk are known both for their Psionic affinity and exceptionally long history, being one of the founding races of the Conclave of Sentience, alongside the Taigron, Redarian, Loriken and Varok-Torividan that still thrive to this day.

**Hykentiu** – Sharks don't typically stand on two legs. But the Hykentiu defy that. Sharks also typically don't walk on land, but the Hykentiu defy that as well. An amphibious species originating from the planet of Kala Bleeg, the Hykentiu are some of the most prolific explorers of all the Conclave species. In fact, the efforts to explore the two sub-oceans that have been observed in the universe are led by Hykentiu research teams, dedicated to figuring out just how to get a vessel into the sub-oceans on Cynofrax or Terevetz without disruptive intrusion. The Astral Expedition League, the most prominent of the universe's stellar exploration guilds, was also founded by a group consisting mostly of Hykentiu adventurers (Of the seventy founding members, sixty-nine of them were Hykentiu).

**Kanikai** – The Kanikai come in a veritable pantheon of different canine breeds, and no one is really sure where the species originated from at first, considering just how many different flavors of Kanikai exist, the actual tracing of their common ancestor species has proven nearly impossible. Among the most common are closely related to the Loriken, like how a husky is closely related to wolves. In most Kanikai circles, the standard form of greeting between friends is to lean against each other until one falls over in the sort of 'push' contest that is the practice of *Ulu-ri poff*, or *Trial By Flop*.

**Laksorian** – Lagomorphs from the planet of Laksor, the Laksorian species are generally a laid back lot, often perfectly content to go with whatever flow the universe is moving at. But this should not present the image of laziness or slack of the Laksorian people, as the Laksorian drive to push the boundaries of knowledge is the stuff of legend. In a way, the Laksorians are masters of the art of working extremely hard to be as lazy as possible. The other most common cause for Laksorians to strive to be the next generation-defining scientist is specifically to prove someone else's atrocious theories wrong, in the sort of 'inspiration by spite' that the Earth 'psychologist' Sigmund Freud famously initiated: By having such absurdly bad and ridiculous theories, entire generations are inspired in the pursuit of proving them wrong.

**Loriken** – A generally polar species, the lupine Loriken more or less come in two types: Reserved, quiet and generally keeping to oneself, or high-energy, outgoing lovers of attention. Of course, there's in between, but in general, one can tell a lot about a Loriken within the first few minutes of meeting one. Generally, Lorikens consider their culturally central planet to be either Kalisaine or Orvitaire, but never Sharaeine, the planet they originated from. No self-respecting Loriken ever considers Sharaeine to be the planet that everyone should think of when thinking about Lorikens.

**Lysanarr** – Feline neighbors to the Taigron, the lion-esque Lysanarr from Gelvetori may not be as outright in their beliefs of honor as the Taigron, but they do hold similar values. To quote former Haji-Son Exemplar Szhen Val'Deyl, "If you were to pay great insult to a Taigron and a Lysanarr simultaneously, both would be equally affronted as the Taigron drew their sword and the Lsyanarr chuckled at how much of a mistake you just made." Lysanarr are also famed for their mastery of distilling spirits, as their homeworld of Gelvetori has become a massive hub for the libation craft. Accolades from the planet's regular spirit competitions are among, if not the single most prestigious any distillery can attain.

**Redarian** – The ailuridae Redarian species are renowned for both their strong sense of honor and morality, and the fierce upholding of their principles. They have been known to literally exile individuals from calling themselves Redarian for poor ideals and even less moral action thereof, a practice known as *Mele Vir,* or "Exile the Name." Many of the most successful battlefield commanders in all of the universe's history were Redarians, as their knack for analytical skills and tactics naturally create genius-level strategists. Naturally, tabletop strategy gaming is a very common form of recreation among the species, and just about every Redarian has a favorite maneuver, that they often name after themselves.

**Taigron** – Despite being a feline species, the Taigron are not actually from the same common ancestor as either the Aliken Sor or Nuberi Felinians, being their own unique evolution from Elas'Sotheel. Fiercely honorable and protective of their friends, these tiger-like warriors from the Altorivian Stride solar system are experts at the delivering of justice and vengeance alike, evinced by their staunch intolerance of the Nuremberg Defense ("I was just following orders"), and any regard of the sin of omission, considering both to be capital crimes. If you ever need to teach someone a painful lesson in how they should *not* tolerate intolerance, and then see the heads of the intolerant subsequently roll, you enlist the aid of a Taigron.

**Varok-Torividan** – When the Primal Draconian species split off into two biological paths, one resulted in the Bol'Drakkin Draconians. The other was the snake-like Varok-Torividan, who are some of the most forthcoming and truthful individuals one will ever meet. According to one Loriken biologist, "A Varok-Torividan will never lie to you, because they wouldn't consider it worth the energy to keep up. If one wanted to stab you, they'd first tell you that they want to stab you, then stab you about ten seconds later if you're still being a jackass. If they were gonna stab you in the back, it would only be because you turned around after learning of their desire to stab you." Two variants of Varok-Torividan exist, the only physical difference being whether they walk on two legs, or are 'hybro-morphic,' where despite having an entirely serpentine body, they still possess arms and prefer to stand upright.

**Vulpian** – The Vulpians are, as their name would suggest, a vulpine species originally hailing from Cynofrax, but have spread out across the stars into nine recognized variants: the tall, more Psionically-inclined Cynofraxians, the Talvas (sometimes referred to as the Dwarven Variant, given their shorter, stockier stature, and knack for engineering and technology), the Death Worlders, renowned for their durability and survival skills, and the genetic offshoots of each: the Crimsonian, descendant from the Cynofrax Vulpians, known for being red in fur color, the Bendorkin, legendary for their agility, and the Lørkas, whose capacity for shenanigans is nigh unparalleled across the cosmos. From the Talvas Vulpians descended the Noregenas, known well for their bouncy demeanor and high energy, and the Dor-Val-Der, whose weapon forging capabilities have been called the stuff of nightmares, to the point where they created the Order of the Perawls, who guard the secrets of the construction of the most dangerous machinations of Dor-Val-Der engineering. The Death Worlders share their closest genetic cousins with the Zharekai Vulpians, the main between them difference being which planet they're from.

**Woran Cos** – A highly Psionically inclined avian species from the planet Teyn-Var-Wolk, the Woran Cos are famed artificers and archaeologists, and the Museum of Archaeotech is the single largest of its kind known to exist, showcasing pieces all the way from the Third Cosmic Era. Like the Corvuseine, Woran Cos naturally possess a pair of functioning wings, though admittedly the Woran Cos are more open towards carrying single passengers on their backs for transportation or thrill rides. Or in some particularly feisty cases, swooping down on an unsuspecting friend and carrying them into the air for an amusing prank.

# GENERAL INFORMATION AND TRIVIA

- On Raon-Arashal, the slang term "Ayen" or "Særin" carries the meaning of "I respectfully acknowledge what you have just said, but I am far too inebriated to say anything else at risk of insult." with "Særin" signifying much more severe inebriation than just "Ayen."

- Miles Radien built a house for himself not far from Torvaltyne Bastion on Raon-Arashal after re-declaring his citizenship from Cynofrax to Raon-Arashal. This house is known as 'The House of the Hecking Borf.' It is rumored to be somewhere within the Blizzardblade Mountains, as it is known that Radien enjoys the aesthetic of a house in the mountains. However, the house itself is not actually an outdoor structure, it is built within a cave in the region, because if there's any aesthetic Radien enjoys more than a mountain house, it's a mountain cave lair.

- The Corvuseine home world of !leysa often holds tournaments for improvised throwing weapons, placing continually more and more ridiculous and impractical thrown implements in the hands of competitors to be thrown with accuracy. One such weapon was called the "Iron hunk." which only four individuals managed to hit the target with.

- The prehensile tails of the Taigron and Lysanarr species have been known to be capable of throwing knives. It's mostly a party trick, however, given that the knife is often only barely held on to, and any parrying motion would quickly disarm the knife-wielding tail.

- Arakai Selendica violently refuses to learn how to play the song 'Wonderwall' on any of the instruments he is versed in. In fact, there was almost an interspecies incident after a Human suggested he play it while he was attending a communal bonfire, and Arakai got exceptionally close to stabbing the Human on the spot.

- The Haji-Son Philanthropic Organization has the official Statement of Aim as "Betterment of Societies." To this end, the HSPO has made it their primary operating principle, the elimination of capitalism across the universe. Their favored tactic is to traverse from world to world, searching for ones "Infected with disease that is the exponential excess of mercantilism, to the rabid and caustic degree that burns and destroys all souls, whether good or bad alike, facilitated by what is even worse than either could ever dream of being in the darkest realms" Despite the apparent wordiness of their mission, the planets they incur upon have yet to fail to meet the definitions of capitalism, as established both by themselves and by reasonable species across the galaxies. Among their most famous operations is the "Tungsten Incursion" on the planet of Malkorasas XI, where the resident mints of the planet utilized tungsten as the metal stamped upon for the standardized currency. As such, the mint held a policy of buying tungsten from any seller, whether miner or scrapper alike. The HSPO, having caught wind of Malkorasas XI's capitalist economic system, utilized the Keystone Forge they had access to, as well as their deep-cover operatives, to "Beam down to the planet and freely hand out ingots of tungsten, one of our operatives legendarily saying 'You get a tungsten bar! And you get a tungsten bar! Is that a tungsten bar in your pants, or are you just happy to see me, you might say? Well guess what, it's not a tungsten bar, it's *two* tungsten bars! And you can have them both!'"

- Almost, if not every town on the planet of Orvitaire has an arena that anyone is free to enter and test their skills in. For every person a combatant either renders unconscious or forces to yield on grounds of 'dead by rights,' they earn a set amount of the local currency per incapacitation.

- The planet of Leresaine, Bolorous, which was not far from the Loriken origin planet of Sharaeine was destroyed in the Fourth Cosmic Era, during a conflict known as the Wars of Chain. However, the planet was uninhabited at the time, so nobody paid much attention. It is believed that the Shard aggressors intended to destroy Sharaeine, but got their information wrong on which planet actually had the Lorikens on it. This ended up giving the Lorikens of Sharaeine the time they needed to prepare a successful defense against the Shard in the conflict that inevitably led to the Sentience War.

- Among Miles Radien's 'Autotelekinetic Cantrips' is a technique he calls 'remote headpats,' where he telekinetically pats a random passerby on the head, leaving them none the wiser on the perpetrator's identity. However, Micah Jorvask almost immediately figured it out after Radien tested this maneuver on her, and subsequently demanded actual headpats at the point of her longsword, as well as supplemental cheek and belly rubs to make up for the attempted coversion.

- One of the fabled Archaeotech artifacts is known as The Blade of Destinaargh, which despises being associated with the concept of destiny so much, to the point that anyone who attempts to say aloud "The Blade of (such)" finds themselves stabbed in the throat by the sword, which is consequently named after the sound people tend to make when this happens, "The Blade of Destin-aargh!" However, it is known that simply referring to it as The Blade of Destinaargh is perfectly safe, as if the weapon is intuitively aware of who is attempting to affront it by associating it with destiny.

- Many have speculated and theorized the name of Jarrek Wöllschlager's claymore, to the point that the Redarian Arch-

Militant has even endorsed a prize to whoever guesses it correctly. Jarrek never actually named his claymore, however.

- The Conclave of Sentience imposes a ban on 'Obnoxious Weapons Technology as well as the common sense ban on nuclear, chemical and biological warfare. Per the Conclave's wording on the ruling's preface, "*To outlaw the use of atomic radiation in warfare is obvious. To forbid biological and chemical warfare is common sense. But the Conclave recognizes also that there is a difference between progress, and the pursuit of making all things drab, dull and lifelessly boring. Though war is never to be prayed for, and not all forms of battle can promise glory, let alone deliver, the Conclave does enact this legislature that combative technologies, such as weapons, armors, and items to boost or enhance their effectiveness, whose effectiveness is beyond reason to the point of obnoxiousness and giggling contempt for one's foes, shall not be utilized. The Spirit of the Stone understands that good men and women don't need rules to tell them to be decent, and though warfare is warfare, and combat is combat, opponents are to be treated like opponents, and not insects to be stomped and swept aside.*" The weapons and defensive implements considered obnoxious, and thus outlawed include landmines, autonomous warfare, and automatic sentry guns with a range greater than 109 meters.

- It is notoriously easy to accidentally flirt with members of the Hajikahl species, as the number of otherwise casual statements or comments they consider compliments is higher than some people have a number for. This includes but is not limited to comments about being tall, comments about being short, comments about being fluffy (which they are), holding out your hand palm-up, comments about eye color, comments about fur pattern, comments about having large handpaws, comments about having small handpaws, literally any metaphor that compares them to fire (since they are natural Pyrokinetics, such comments are particularly potent), and being flustered at how easy it is to accidentally flirt with a Hajikahl. Apparently, even the mere act of obviously being deliberate with your speech so as not to accidentally flirt with them is itself considered a form of flirting.

- Draconians of the Bol'Drakkin Genetic Caste have a fifty-fifty chance of being born with toe beans, akin to most species that have paws rather than claws. One of Miles Radien's favorite pranks to pull on one such Dragon at the Fortress Borfus is to poke the Shipyard Maintenance Chief's beans.

- The recognized anthem of both the planets Redaria Prime and Redaria Omega is simply titled "Redaria." Though it consists of only four lines, it is among the most recognizable of the planetary anthems, which tend to fall into the trap of being overly grand and complex. The hymn itself is "*Kiar at-al, le arenal bole redah tiadoremal. Perve se-al tin le tor-al, kelasten vore zalos tival. Mele sendir, le ste te vir, yanpal satul ketar raiyaan. Tor elanah, stennal korah, vaikaisura, Redaria!*" which translates roughly as "Unity eternal in the champions of (the) red suns, tainted never by the exemplars of darkness cursing our midst, exile them by steel and cross out their names that we become wisdom at last, lead with honor and be not affronting, be who you are, Redarians!" Though this is not an exact translation, it is a translation of the message it conveys.

- The planetary flag of the Lørkas Vulpian homeworld of Piar Kel is an infamously bad design for a flag. Some have theorized that this was the intent of the Lørkas Vulpians, as they are just as well known for this sort of thing.

- The Kanikai slang term *Muhl-Muhl* is often used as an exasperated remark for when someone has a sudden bout of comical incompetency. *Muhl* is also the Common Borktongue (the most universal of the Kanikai languages) word for "Moon." and the phrase itself is typically construed as *Balf olf, muhl-muhl,* or "God dammit, moon moon."

- The Death World Vulpians of Raon-Arashal have an entire genre of music called *Volkarn Orkest*, or "Battle Anthems." songs to be played in battle to pump up spirits and get the blood flowing. After the Human species was introduced to the wider universe, some Earth bands and musicians found themselves spiking in popularity on Raon-Arashal for basically being creators of *Volkarn Orkests,* most commonly Symphonic Power Metal and Finnish Industrial Metal groups.

www.ingramcontent.com/pod-product-compliance
Lightning Source LLC
Chambersburg PA
CBHW070528100726
47907CB00004B/1028

* 9 7 8 1 5 9 0 9 2 9 4 9 0 *